'My name is Andrew.'

Emily looked up into the unreadable depths of his eyes, and made a conscious decision that it wasn't wise to get to know Dr Andrew Dashwood any better.

He smiled. 'I'm sure we'll meet again, Emily. Do I know your fiancé?'

'Yes, I expect you must know Gerald Montague.'

Dashwood's handsome face tensed. 'Yes, I know him. Not well, but enough.'

Emily faced him, sensing danger. 'What do you mean?'

Dear Reader

We continue with our quartet, LONG HOT SUMMER, in which Babs starts work in the rehabilitation unit, and complete the Lennox duet with LEGACY OF SHADOWS, where Christy has to face her past. Jenny Ashe takes us to Singapore, an area she knows well, in IN THE HEAT OF THE SUN, and from Caroline Anderson we have PICKING UP THE PIECES. Nick, in her previous book SECOND THOUGHTS, demanded his own story, and this is it. Just what you need in cold February to warm you. Enjoy!

The Editor

Lancashire-born, **Jenny Ashe** read English at Birmingham, returned home with a BA and rheumatoid arthritis. Married in Scotland to a Malaysian-born junior surgeon, she returned to Liverpool with three Scottish children when her husband became a GP in 1966. She has written non-stop since then—articles, short stories, radio talks, and novels. She considers the medical environment compassionate, fascinating and completely rewarding.

Recent titles by the same author:

SWEET DECEIVER
THE STORM AND THE PASSION

IN THE HEAT OF THE SUN

BY
JENNY ASHE

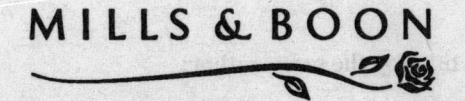

MILLS & BOON

MILLS & BOON LIMITED
ETON HOUSE, 18–24 PARADISE ROAD
RICHMOND, SURREY, TW9 1SR

All the characters in this book have no existence outside the imagination of the Author, and have no relation whatsoever to anyone bearing the same name or names. They are not even distantly inspired by any individual known or unknown to the Author, and all the incidents are pure invention.

All Rights Reserved. The text of this publication or any part thereof may not be reproduced or transmitted in any form or by any means, electronic or mechanical, including photocopying, recording, storage in an information retrieval system, or otherwise, without the written permission of the publisher.

This book is sold subject to the condition that it shall not, by way of trade or otherwise, be lent, resold, hired out or otherwise circulated without the prior consent of the publisher in any form of binding or cover other than that in which it is published and without a similar condition including this condition being imposed on the subsequent purchaser.

*First published in Great Britain 1994
by Mills & Boon Limited*

© Jenny Ashe 1994

*Australian copyright 1994
Philippine copyright 1994
This edition 1994*

ISBN 0 263 78473 8

*Set in 10 on 11½ pt Linotron Times
03-9402-56433*

*Typeset in Great Britain by Centracet, Cambridge
Made and printed in Great Britain*

CHAPTER ONE

THE skyscrapers of Singapore towered elegantly into the hazy blue of a sweltering tropical sky. The palm trees along Orchard Road looked artificial in their perfection, as did the exotic flower arrangements in the hotel foyer — yellow chrysanthemums as big as dinner plates, and graceful white and magenta orchids. Gleaming chrome, thick carpets and oriental ornaments, the high white ceilings with lamps shaped like lanterns, and the crystal chandeliers — Emily Fairlie looked around at all the luxury, and wondered how the people could just carry on a normal business day amid such splendour. Yet the men in their lightweight suits and women in smart skirts and blouses bustled around Emily, and the few tourists who were around at nine in the morning looked out of place in their casual shorts, sandals and gaudy shirts.

One man suddenly caught her full attention, as she sat demurely waiting for Gerald, an untouched cup of coffee on the table beside her. Idly swinging one slim foot in its new fashionable shoe, she had been watching the people in the foyer, the courteous staff, the sprightly bell-boys and the imposing dark-skinned doorman in an elaborate Indian turban set with a large jewel. Then it happened. The man who walked in made the usually reticent Emily stare. He was taller than the Chinese and Malay people around him, and his tanned face with its fine features and waving brown hair was the handsomest Emily had ever seen, striking and electrifying, as though a film star had just entered the lobby. She watched, fascinated, as he strode through the door held by the doorman, and paused to thank him, and exchange a word or two with him. He must be a regular. Or did he work here? Gerald did too. Maybe they would meet. . .

He was coming nearer to her, and Emily tried to look away. But she was a split-second too late, and he caught her staring. For what seemed like an age, they looked at one another, and she demurely lowered her eyes. His light blue eyes were magnetic, and he knew it. His figure was slim but muscular beneath the white silk shirt and dark grey tailored trousers. His dark tie was expensive, like his Rolex watch, and his black shoes reflected the crystal of the chandeliers. This was no tourist. He belonged here. Emily felt a thrill of anticipation because soon she would belong here too, and it felt good.

It was cool in the lobby, the efficient air-conditioning making the atmosphere a comfortable contrast with the aching heat outside. Yet Emily found her hands sweating, her body warm with some unknown reaction, as though the sun had walked into the lobby with the man.

And then he had carried on walking. She didn't turn her head, although she was curious. But she was waiting here for her fiancé, Gerald Montague, and she knew she was one of the luckiest girls in the world to have been chosen by the wealthy and powerful businessman. Dear Gerald. She was longing to see him again — they had been apart for five months already, and the time had dragged, even though she had worked extra shifts to pass the time.

The telephone had rung discreetly at the gleaming desk, and one of the immaculate Chinese receptionists came out towards her. 'You are Miss Fairlie, madam?'

'Yes, how did you know?'

'Mr Montague was on the line—he described you very well, madam—slim, long fair hair and grey eyes. There is no one else remotely like that at the moment.' She smiled. 'Mr Montague asked me to let you know that he is unfortunately detained again at the bank. He asked me to make his apologies. He hopes to be here before ten, but it may be longer.'

'Then I might as well do a little sightseeing. Thank you.' Emily picked up her purse. Gerald was always busy. Even when she landed last night, he had sent his chauffeur for her rather than meet her himself. She had been in Singapore one night, and, though Gerald had written so often that she felt she knew it well, the actual city was beginning to exceed all her expectations. There was an atmosphere, an excitement in the air, a feeling of dynamism, of confidence and of promise. Emily paused on her way to the door. Was it Singapore that had brought on these feelings? Or was it perhaps the chance meeting with that very handsome young man that had made her life suddenly much more interesting? No, that was impossible. Emily was as good as engaged, and had thought of little else but Gerald since he had kissed her goodbye at Heathrow Airport and flown back to Singapore five months ago.

The heat of the tropical morning met her like a wall as Emily approached the open door. 'You wish for a taxi, madam?' The doorman in his smart white uniform, with gold epaulettes and cloth-of-gold turban, was already holding the door wide for her. A large blue Mercedes was just drawing up outside. Suddenly it swerved and skidded, as though the driver had lost control. Fortunately it was almost stationary, and it came to a halt against a tall weeping fig in a Chinese marble vase.

Both Emily and the doorman ran to the driver's seat,

where the man inside was slumped over the steering-wheel. The doorman switched off the engine, and pulled on the handbrake. 'Call a doctor, madam, please! He's unconscious.'

'I'm a nurse. Let me see to him while you call a doctor.' She was already pulling him straight, and leaning him back against the seat. She felt the pulse in his neck — he was sweating and the heartbeat was present, but faint. His lips had a bluish tinge. It looked very much like a cardiac infarction. He was the right type, too — overweight and florid, with a cigar in the ashtray beside him, and a thick file of papers on the other seat.

Emily looked up to get some help, sweat already running down her face from her exertions. The poor man needed to lie flat. There was already a circle of onlookers between the marble plant-pots and the elaborate chrysanthemums, and as she looked the spectators parted. To her consternation it was the handsome man with the blue eyes who came elbowing through with a look of confidence on his face, and a stethoscope in his hand. He blotted out the sun for a moment before kneeling to see to the patient. 'It's Mahmoud. I might have known,' he murmured to himself in a deep, velvety voice, as he took a small sphygmomanometer from his pocket, and swiftly read the unconscious man's blood-pressure. So he was a doctor. She had guessed him to be someone influential.

Again she felt uncomfortably warm, but there was no time for her palpitations now. She stood back for him to bend over the stricken man. She said calmly, 'An infarct, I think. Could be a big one, Doctor? Respiration's very ragged — the heart is fibrillating, and pulse is very faint.'

He didn't turn from his examination, but his smooth,

cultured voice sounded relieved. 'You're medical? Thank goodness. Let's get him on a stretcher!' He beckoned, and two porters helped him lift the man gently down, and carried him into the hotel, out of the oppressive heat of the sun and into the cool air-conditioned interior. 'No, not here. We mustn't upset the guests.' The doctor had his hand on the wrist of the patient, monitoring his pulse, as they swiftly removed the drama away from the eyes of the prying public and into the quiet calm of the hotel's medical room.

The cool young doctor wasted no more time. He had already taken the blood-pressure, and now he listened carefully to the heartbeat. Then he reached in his medical case and took out a phial of atropine. The patient had once opened his eyes, groaned, and closed them again. Emily wiped his brow gently with a cotton pad, and held his hand, as his breathing gradually became steadier, and he opened his eyes again.

'What happened?' he asked.

The doctor felt for a vein, and smoothly injected the atropine. As he withdrew the needle, Emily was ready with a pad of gauze to put pressure on the injection site until the bleeding stopped. The doctor murmured, as he put the used needle carefully away, 'You collapsed, Mahmoud. Don't worry. I'll get you to the hospital, and we'll soon have you comfortable.'

The competent words, spoken in that reassuring tone, had a dramatic effect on the patient. Hoarsely, but less breathless now, he said, 'Oh, it's you, Dashwood. Lucky for me, lah!' He closed his eyes again, and winced as he shifted on the stretcher. His voice sank to a husky whisper. 'Thanks for — not saying I told you so. Are you taking me to Mount Elizabeth?'

'If you wish. It's the nearest. But I don't work there. I only have beds in the Ambassador.'

The Ambassador! That was the hospital Emily had applied to — the hospital she would soon be working in. She flushed again, and wondered whether to mention it. But there was no time. The patient was whispering hoarsely, 'Then I'll — go to the — Ambassador. Get — my secretary to phone my wife, there's a — good chap.'

Emily said quietly, 'Shall I do that, Dr Dashwood?'

For the first time Dashwood turned and acknowledged her presence with a slight smile of appreciation. 'Would you, please? His company phone number is here, on his notebook.' As she reached for it, and went to the desk to take the phone, he added, looking straight at her now, 'And thank you for your help.'

She felt warm with her efforts, and a little embarrassed at his approbation. 'You're welcome.' She dialled the number.

While she held on, Dr Dashwood said with more personal interest now, 'You have a name?'

'Sister Fairlie.'

The doctor smiled slightly. 'Ah, it's not first-name time, then? We have already met, though. I distinctly recall seeing you as I came in this morning, and do you know, Sister Fairlie, I had an idea that you noticed me?'

So she had made an impression on him, then, in spite of the briefness of the moment when they first set eyes on one another. He had certainly made an impression on her, and she was trying hard to deny it to herself. She was an engaged woman, and any fleeting attraction was totally unimportant. Emily had come to Singapore to be with Gerald, and she had no need to remind herself how much she had missed him.

The ringing phone was answered by Mr Mahmoud's secretary then, and Emily quickly explained what had happened. 'And he is being transferred to the

Ambassador Clinic at once. No, he is not in immediate danger. Dr Dashwood was on the spot.' She looked at Dashwood. 'The address of the Ambassador? It's Edinburgh Place, isn't it?'

He smiled again. 'They'll know, Sister. Everybody knows the Ambassador. So you aren't a tourist? I took you for one when I first spotted you in the lobby.'

She tried not to notice the lazy charm of his smile, the way his eyes brightened, those very blue eyes that mirrored the blue of the sky. She said impersonally, 'I'm new. It's my first day in this country. But I've heard of the Ambassador.' This country of flowers and skyscrapers, of elegant women and wealthy men, of overwhelming warmth and an exciting *frisson* of mystery. . . She replaced the phone, and went back to the patient. She said to the doctor, 'Would you like me to go with him to the hospital?'

'Thanks very much, but no. He's an old friend of mine, a fellow member of the cricket club. I'll take him.' He turned to the little receptionist, who had been hovering around them. 'You know where I'll be, Amy? I've got my phone.' He pointed to the mobile phone clipped to his back pocket.

'Thank you, Doctor.'

Dashwood nodded, and turned back to Emily. 'That was very decent of you, offering to give up your time for a total stranger. Are you here on holiday?'

There was no reason why she had to tell him anything about herself, but somehow it seemed right to make it clear she wasn't free. 'Oh, no. I've come to join my fiancé. We're to be married here.'

His face and attractive voice were both totally impassive. 'Then I can only wish you every happiness, and thank you again, Sister Fairlie.'

The ambulancemen came in then, and quietly and

efficiently carried the limp body of the businessman out to the waiting private ambulance. Emily watched them go. Dr Dashwood paused in the door of the medical room, after putting his case away, and held out his hand to Emily. She took it, finding his grip firm and his handshake just a fraction longer than was needed. Again she found her gaze drawn to his face, the speaking blue eyes with thick, straight brows, the smooth cheeks and perfectly sculpted jaw. Holding that life-saving hand, she did her best to hide the interest in her eyes and the tinge of pink in her face at meeting her future colleague.

As the ambulance was driving away along the circular drive towards the busy road, Dr Dashwood gave Emily a little wave of gratitude, as he settled himself at the side of his patient, and the doors swung to. The palm trees seemed to hover in a haze, their fronded leaves suspended in the palpable heat. Emily's right hand was just slightly raised in reply, when a petulant voice said, 'Well, I didn't expect my fiancée to be waving to another man.'

She turned. 'Gerald! Oh, Gerald.' And she flung herself into his arms, her embrace warmer than she had intended.

Mollified by her welcome, he said, 'Didn't think you'd be so pleased to see me, old thing. My, you're shaking. Don't tell me—you were helping to see to Mahmoud, weren't you? They were saying he had a heart attack on the doorstep. Trust you to want to help. Nervous reaction, is it, this shaking? Never off duty, my little fiancée! You know, Emily, once we're married, you'll be a society wife, and I'm going to teach you how to do it perfectly. No time to go ministering to the sick. Your career isn't going to matter half as much as being with me.'

'Of course, darling,' Emily said. She was an honest girl and she meant it—life had been quite empty without him, and it had seemed easy to give in her notice and write for the job at the Ambassador. But her tone was hollow. She wanted him, but she wanted her nursing as well—just for a while. Gerald knew very well how much her work meant to her. Old arguments about it in England came back to haunt her, and now he was emphasising his point of view yet again. He wanted a wife to be a hostess for him, a mistress of the social graces and an epitome of beauty and grace. Emily was aware that one of the reasons he was first attracted to her was her wealth of naturally fair hair. He made no secret of the fact that his wife would be a reflection of his own success and good taste. Hence her smart blue linen suit and these expensive shoes, which, she noted with alarm, had been scuffed rather badly during her ministrations to Mr Mahmoud.

'I think maybe you need a drink to calm you down, sweet. I wouldn't mind one myself—I've had a hard time arguing with the bank to let me have another loan for expansion of the health club.'

'It's a bit early, Gerald.' With all the fuss of the incident, Emily hadn't noticed the time until now. 'It's only eleven.'

He smiled, with a superior lift of an eyebrow. 'This country is Libertyville, Emily. So long as you stick to their rules, you can do what you like when you like. And you need a drink.'

'No, truly I don't. I'm quite used to emergencies, you know, Gerry.' Her heartbeat was returning to normal now, and she was looking up at Gerald, remembering just how darkly good looking he was, and how safe and cared-for he made her feel.

'Then why were you trembling?'

'Oh—just everything—being here, being too hot—and it was so sudden, Mahmoud's collapse.'

He put an arm around her shoulders and hugged her. 'That's true, and you aren't used to the heat. We'll go up to my office to cool down. Plenty of time—we aren't meeting Foo until one.'

Gerald's palatial office and suite of rooms was on the first floor, beside some very expensive dress and shoe shops, and a svelte physiotherapy and exercise hall. Emily watched him as he opened a Queen Anne cabinet and produced two crystal tumblers. He instinctively knew what was the right thing to do, and Emily had always admired that trait in her fiancé. As he poured the best whisky from a crystal decanter, and added bottled water to hers, Emily studied with new eyes the man she had promised—and for whom she had given up her life, friends and job in England—to marry.

He wasn't as tall as Dr Dashwood, but still above the average height for Singapore. He had a neatly styled head of glossy dark hair, keen, rather narrow brown eyes, and a Roman nose. Anyone looking at him would be sure he was an aristocrat and a man of power. He wore a waistcoat over a fitted shirt, obviously well-tailored to his very outline, a dark spotted silk tie, and shark-skin trousers in dark blue. He had a matching jacket slung over the back of his chair behind the desk. Yes, as everyone had told her in England, the Honourable Gerald St Clair Montague was quite a catch for a nursing sister who was the daughter of an unassuming country vet. She had been flattered by his attentions, and found it easy to fall in love with his boyish charm and impeccable manners.

Gerald turned and smiled at her as he handed her the glass. She noticed that when he stretched his tailored shirt pulled slightly at the buttons. Gerald was putting on weight. Yet she couldn't blame him—quite obviously it was impossible not to live the high life when moving in these circles. It appeared that he too had been looking his fiancée over. 'You're looking lovely, sweetie. I like the little suit—but I must get Annabel to take you for some real clothes.' The condescending tone was slight, but it was there. And who on earth was Annabel?

She found herself unable to find a suitable reply. Real clothes? She had never spent so much on a suit before... Back in England, Gerald was always the most tactful of men. She said quietly, 'I didn't bring much. I knew I would have you to advise me.'

He sipped his drink before smiling down at her as she sat on his luxurious leather swivel chair. 'First things first, darling. After lunch—sorry about it, but I'd arranged to meet Foo ages ago, and he's a billionaire I can't put off, so I'm afraid it's a business lunch—after that, I'm taking you to the best diamond merchant in Singapore. You are having the engagement ring we never got round to buying in Britain.' He held out his hand, and she put her left hand in it. 'Yes, these pretty fingers are for precious stones—they weren't made for bedpans. The beautician here in the hotel can do your manicures, but I think for facials and hair Annabel will know the best. How are you for cash? Here, just for pocket money'—— he took out a wad of hundred-dollar bills and handed them to her—'buy anything you wish my sweet, within reason. But wait for decent outfits until Annabel can come with you.'

Emily felt a little uncomfortable. She had never been one for allowing anyone to take over her life, and she felt she had to stand up for a trace of independence. Gerald was steamrollering her—first about not nursing again, and now about her clothes and her appearance.

She sat up straight and suggested, 'Darling, if your business lunch was already arranged, why don't you leave me out of it? I'd like to rest a while after that business with Mr Mahmoud. Pick me up later? Please?'

Gerald looked hard at her. 'You're not afraid of meeting my business friends? Is that why——?'

'Certainly not. I'm looking forward to meeting all your circle. But I think you wanted to test my social graces at your lunch today, didn't you, Gerry? I'm jet-lagged, remember, and awfully hot. I'm sure I wouldn't do either of us justice.'

He didn't seem pleased, but he read the determination in her clear grey eyes. 'OK, my sweet.' Gerald drew her up into his arms. 'Oh, I've missed your warm little body.' He kissed her, and for a moment she felt secure, as in the old days. It would all be fine, once she had settled in. But then she drew away from him.

'What's the matter now?'

She thought fast. 'Sorry, darling—I spent ages on my make-up this morning. I wanted to impress you. You don't want lipstick on your collar.'

'It looks very natural to me.'

'That's the art, you see.'

Gerald looked at his large diamond-studded Swiss watch. 'I can't say I'd mind a spot of lipstick when it's yours, sweetheart. But I'd better give Reception a call to get my limo and driver ready. You'll go to your room and rest, you say?'

'I will, just as soon as you go.'

'Want me to get them to send up some smoked salmon?'

'I'll ring if I want anything.'

'OK, sweetie. Then we'll leave things like that.'

Emily watched him go, wondering why she had drawn back from him.

* * *

Emily knew why she wanted to be alone. She was shocked with herself for not being a hundred per cent delighted to be reunited with her perfect fiancé. A man in a million, a woman's dream, the most eligible man in London. They had met when she nursed him in an exclusive private hospital in London. She had never actually told him that she was only doing agency nursing there to do a sick friend a favour. Moonlighting, but only to help poor Angela keep her job. They had used to meet at his company flat near Marble Arch, and Gerald had shown no interest in her work. Gerald had never asked, and she never told him, that she had been a top sister in the neuro department of the Royal Lester, in Brixton, where most of the patients came from deprived backgrounds, and she had been happy to use her qualities of understanding and compassion to the full, as well as her nursing skill.

She went down to the lobby with him to see Gerald off, and received a lot of covert attention from the staff, who she knew had been longing to find out what kind of girl the Honourable Gerald was going to marry. He bent and kissed her cheek before getting into his white Mercedes beside his Chinese driver. Inside she felt pride, excitement, relief at being reunited. But also she felt sad, because he had sounded so certain that she would give up nursing. . . It was a disappointing moment. Eight thousand miles she had travelled for this man, giving up her job for one in Singapore to be close to him. It wasn't going to be easy to admit that it might all have gone wrong. She watched as the car purred its way round the circular drive, under the tall palm trees and the bright flowerbeds, and out into the heat and the Singapore traffic.

Emily felt guilt, relief and bewilderment all at once. Maybe it would take a few days for her to feel comfortable with Gerald again. Maybe there was nothing to worry about really. Life stretched ahead of her, a fabulous life if she chose it, where she would lack nothing money could buy, and live in this paradise of trees and flowers and diamonds.

'Hello again, Sister.'

She jumped, before saying breathlessly, 'Oh, Dr Dashwood!'

'You look startled.'

'I was daydreaming.' She knew she was flattered by his attention, the way he had made a bee-line for her when he came in. 'You're back quickly.'

'Mahmoud's in good hands at the Ambassador. And today is my day to be here.'

Very aware that the staff had been watching her with Gerald, and were probably still watching her with Dashwood, she said, 'I must be going.' It would be foolhardy to make a poor impression on her first day.

'Don't rush off. It's too hot.' They stood motionless for a moment, hotel guests bustling about them in search of food and drink, before he said, 'I was going for a spot of lunch. Maybe you'd allow me to buy you lunch, to thank you for looking after my patient?'

She tried to hide a slight smile. But he noticed, and she had to explain, 'I've just told my fiancé that I don't want lunch. It would be quite wrong to go off with — to see me — oh, you know what I mean!'

'He wouldn't believe that medical people often lunch together?' The young doctor was showing persistence, and Emily felt apprehension because he was looking at her with something like admiration.

Emily looked down. Now would be the time to tell him that she was going to work at the Ambassador. But she was well aware of her own sudden admiration for this young man's medical skill as well as his looks, and her main preoccupation was to get rid of him before he noticed it. 'I did say no, thank you.'

He said gravely, 'I see. Your fiancé wouldn't understand.'

How did he know that? 'Exactly. So, Dr——'

'My name is Andrew.'

She looked up into the unreadable depths of his eyes, and made a conscious decision that it wasn't wise to get to know Andrew Dashwood any better. 'Emily.' In a very low voice.

He smiled. 'I'll take myself off, then. I'm sure we'll meet again, Emily. Do I know your fiancé? Does he have an office here?'

'Yes, he does. I expect you must know Gerald Montague.'

Dr Dashwood's handsome face tensed, and he took a step back. He tried to keep his voice level, but she felt a surge of hidden anger in him as he said smoothly, 'Montague! Yes, I do know him. Not well, but enough.'

Alarmed, she faced him, sensing danger. 'What do you mean? Enough for what?'

He looked down at her, and for a second he reached out and touched a lock of her hair very lightly as it lay on her shoulder. 'It doesn't matter. Just as well you told me, and a good thing we didn't do lunch. I must be going.'

'But——'

He had regained his composure. Standing square before her, he once again took her hand politely, again holding it fractionally longer than was strictly necessary. 'Goodbye, Sister Fairlie.' Her fingers tingled at his pressure, while the doctor strode towards the medical room, his eyes lowered.

Emily went up to her room with a thoughtful frown. This episode was deeply alarming. The doctor she was going to be working with already disliked her fiancé. And her fiancé very clearly disliked her nursing. Even before she had set eyes on the Ambassador Clinic, it was surrounded by problems.

CHAPTER TWO

WHEN Gerald Montague tapped at Emily's hotel room door, it was after six, and she had slept most of the afternoon. She rubbed her eyes, and patted down her tangled hair. She was glad to see him. Maybe things would go right now. He kissed her and smoothed back her hair where she had failed. 'Caught up on your sleep, sweet? Miss me?'

'I did. Oh, Gerald, it is nice to be here with you. I'm glad I came. It's going to be the way it was in London again, isn't it? Did your lunch go well?'

'Pretty well, I hope. You can never tell with some of these people. They smile and call you "friend" to your face, but behind your back they're counting your assets before they invite you to a return lunch.'

Emily looked at him, sensing tension in his reply. 'I suppose your job is pretty high-pressure?'

'And how! It's the health club project — we're expanding fast, and I want to keep up the momentum. Some of the other board members are trying to make too many rules. Worried about the cash flow! I tell you, Emily, I'm just so relieved you're here to help me unwind. Cash flow indeed! Anything to do with physical fitness will take off now, and we must catch the market at the right time! That Dashwood — sorry, Emily, let's forget business for a while. Let's have some champagne in my office.'

Emily's heart gave a lurch. There couldn't be two Dashwoods — he must be talking about Andrew. So they were distinctly at odds over their mutual business interests. She said nothing. There was no need for her to show any interest in Dr Dashwood, even though it was very likely she might meet him again when she reported for work at the Ambassador. . .

They went down in the lift to the first floor, and into the luxury office suite next to the fitness centre. She looked up at the elegant heading over the double glass doors, where in large gold letters was printed 'South East Asia Health Clubs'. Gerald ushered her into his lounge, and soon had a bottle of Bollinger on ice. He kissed Emily again, holding her close. 'Maybe we can make it like London again. But remember, sweet, while I was there, I was on holiday after my appendicitis. Thank God for faxes while I recuperated properly. This is where the hard work is done, the money is made. I'll be busy a lot of the time. It's not going to be easy, darling. It won't be much of a holiday from now on.'

She sensed his warning. Slowly she began to see that she had been tempted to come out here by his promises of the good life. Yet what Gerald really wanted was someone to share his burdens with — someone who would charm his business associates and provide him with comfort and relaxation. It was very different from what she had expected. But Emily wasn't a quitter. She loved Gerald, and didn't want to disappoint him. Brightly she said, 'Tell me, darling, when am I going to see your apartment?'

'I thought we'd move your stuff there tonight.'

Emily stared. 'Move in with you? Oh, but—I couldn't—not yet. You said you would find me a place. You agreed that we would both need a little time to get to know one another again. It was your idea—you kept writing in your letters that our engagement isn't definite until we both decide we want it.'

His dark eyes raked her figure as she stood before

him. 'You mean you came all this way and you still haven't made up your mind, Emily?'

'I came because you made it sound so wonderful. But I didn't come to live on your money—I came to work, darling. I have a job fixed. I thought we could go on seeing each other, as we did in London.' Her voice faltered. 'Please say it's all right, Gerald. It was your idea to have time to get used to each other again.'

He sighed crossly. 'You're right, Emily. It was my idea. But the moment I saw you I knew I didn't need any time. What made you change?'

She took a deep breath and explained quietly, 'I think it was the way you spoke about my work, Gerald.'

'Well, it was a shock. You actually got yourself a job? With a work permit?'

'Yes.'

Gerald swore under his breath. 'You might have told me. So I come second, is that it?'

The old quarrel was beginning, and Emily bit her lip, determined not to lose her temper. 'You've never come second with me, Gerald. You know that. I just happen to have a career that I love—that I'm good at, and I know very well I won't be happy not doing it.' She kept her voice very steady and reasonable. 'You did say you want me to be happy. That way I can be of most use to you.'

'Use? When your shifts coincide with my important meetings? When you are called out just when I need you to advise me—to listen to me—to be my hostess and help me clinch my deals?'

'Of course—yes. I asked for the option of part-time work. Isn't that good enough for you? Let me just start at the clinic, and see how things go?' It was all wrong, suddenly. She shouldn't have to plead for Gerald's permission to do her job. She added more lamely,

'There's no way they can force me to stay if the conditions interfere with our seeing each other.'

Gerald lifted the chilled champagne from the pail, wrapped it in a pure white linen napkin and poured them both a sparkling glass. He was trying not to shout, and she appreciated him trying. He said, 'Why didn't you tell me?'

Emily was honest, her clear grey eyes wide. 'It was a last-minute thing. I saw the advertisement in the London paper, and only heard from the Ambassador a couple of days before I took the flight that they had accepted me.' She knelt at his feet and looked into his eyes. 'Gerald, you know I came out here because of you. I'm staying because of you. But I don't want to stay as a — kept woman, and you know I have no income unless I work.'

'We could get married.'

'It's what I want, too. But for both our sakes we ought to see if I fit into your life as comfortably as I did in London. You said yourself that life is very different here.'

He stood up and drank. His voice was harsh. 'Why the Ambassador?'

'Because they wanted a neuro nurse, and that's my speciality, as you well know.'

He began to pace the room. It was decorated in muted blues and mauves, with a large batik picture of slim brown women in sarongs working in a stylised rubber plantation of tall, thin trees. Emily watched him as he wrestled with his own thoughts. He said at last, 'I thought I had it all, Emily. Money, position, apartment, and a beautiful young wife-to-be. It looks as though I don't.'

She felt wretched at his disappointment. But it wasn't her fault. It was a misunderstanding. She said, 'Don't say it like that. We don't need to wait long. Just long enough for us both to settle down.'

He swung on his heel and looked her straight in the eye. His words pierced her heart. 'You know, I'm beginning to regret asking you to come, Emily. There are girls here who would have jumped at the chance.'

She turned away as though he had hit her. Her voice was very low as she replied, 'It didn't sound like that in your letters. You told me I was the only one for you, Gerald. I wouldn't have thrown up everything for you if I didn't feel the same.'

'You have a funny way of showing it.' He stood facing her. She still sat on the carpet, and now she scrambled to her feet and met his gaze bravely. Gerald said, 'I'm going out. I'll give you a call tomorrow.'

She said, fighting back tears, 'If you wish. But it's not the best way of getting to know one another again, is it?'

'I need to think things over.'

Emily didn't answer. She watched him with sad eyes, as he picked up his jacket and slung it over his shoulder. He paused at the door, and grudgingly admitted, 'You have a point, of course. I did say all that junk in my letters. But somehow I didn't remember you being so strong-minded about things. I believed you would fall in with my wishes.'

'You thought I would be the obedient little woman? Oh, Gerald, you surely know me better than that. The days of Madam Butterfly are over. I love you, but you must take me as I am. I am a nurse, as well as loving you and wanting to be with you. And you wouldn't want me if I had no mind of my own. I'd be even less use to you like that. You'd very soon get tired of me then.'

'You could be right, Emily, but believe me, I know

some very pretty Madam Butterflies who have been making eyes at me for some time. Women with looks, money and breeding.'

It sounded very much as though Gerald was emphasising the fact that Emily had no money of her own. But she tried not to believe he could be so mercenary. She said gently, 'It's all a front, isn't it? I've met women like that. Once they had your gold ring and your front-door key, you know as well as I do who would be in charge. At least I tell you to your face, Gerald, that I need a little independence. I'm being honest with you. Give me credit for that. And—I do love you.'

He closed the door again and turned back to her. 'You swear that?'

'I swear it.'

'And you think you'd be happy being the little woman if I settled for you doing some part-time work?'

'I'm sure of it.'

'Then I'm willing to give it a try, Emily. Come here.' He took her in his arms, and hugged her to him. With his cheek against hers, he whispered, 'I'm sorry I was rude—blame it on pressure.' He went to the coffee-table and poured them both more champagne. 'Go and change, sweetie—we'll have dinner at the Raffles.'

'You don't need to bribe me with treats. It's wonderful just being here. A simple meal would be fine.'

Gerald Montague kissed her again. 'Sensible and frugal too. Emily, I'm falling for you all over again. Don't make me wait too long for your decision?'

She kissed him back, feeling a lot happier. 'We'll both know when the time is right, won't we?'

'Yes, my angel. Now hurry and change. I'm getting hungry.'

* * *

Next morning Emily woke knowing that she couldn't afford to stay here at the Tanglin Palace hotel. Obviously Gerald had made no attempt to find her somewhere to stay, expecting her to go and live with him, and her refusal had angered him a little. If she wanted a place to stay, she must find her own place, and the best way to do that was to find out from the Ambassador Clinic what arrangements they made for their nursing staff.

She breakfasted in her room, and then packed her cases. Taking the Ambassador's letter of acceptance from her things, she dialled the number of the nursing officer. An efficient, cheerful voice answered. 'Hello, Ambassador? Sister Boon here.'

'Sister Boon, good morning. My name is Emily Fairlie, and I——'

'Oh, Sister Fairlie, how nice to talk to you. I've been expecting your call. Would you like to come along this morning to meet us? I'm free at eleven.'

'Thank you very much.'

'I believe you went to the assistance of Mr Mahmoud? We are all talking about it. You'll be glad to hear he's coming along very well.'

'That's good news, Sister Boon.' Emily already had a good opinion of the Ambassador, after the pleasant letter from their neuro department offering her a job. Sister Boon reinforced her good opinion. She wasted no time in calling for a porter to take her things downstairs. Then she took the roll of banknotes Gerald had given her, and sealed it in an envelope, which she posted through the door of Gerald's office as she passed it. She ought never to have taken it. She would spend in Singapore only the money she had earned herself.

Emily couldn't help noticing that the health club was busy, with lissom young women in leotards lounging in the foyer, and bronzed businessmen emerging after what appeared to be a regular morning work-out. The health business was booming. She agreed with Gerald on that. What objections could Andrew Dashwood have to the company expanding while it had the chance?

Handing her key in at Reception, Emily paid her bill. 'I'll send for my luggage later today.'

'Certainly. Have you a forwarding address, madam?'

She hadn't. 'But I can be contacted through the Ambassador Clinic?'

'Really? So you must know Dr Dashwood? I thought it was only a coincidence that you gave him assistance when Mr Mahmoud was taken ill. But you knew him already.'

Emily didn't go into details. Memories of that hectic episode, of her first disturbing sight of the good-looking young doctor, flooded into her consciousness, blotting out for a moment her thoughts of her fiancé. 'I hadn't met the doctor before. But I'm glad I was able to help. Good morning.'

'Thank you, madam. Good morning. Have a nice day.'

Out in the sunshine, Emily was reminded with a jolt of the utter heat of the tropics. Even with air-conditioning inside, and the lush vegetation around the hotel gardens, she was reminded just how cruel the sun could be, and how quickly she wanted to be out of its searching rays. The taxi called by the Sikh with the turban was blessedly cool, its air-conditioning at full blast. 'Ambassador Clinic, please.'

In five minutes she was there. So this was her place of work! It looked more like yet another classy hotel. Emily was dropped at the ornate white pillared doorway, with marble steps up to the mahogany doors.

Inside it was hushed and elegant, exuding style and taste. White flowers, mostly orchids and chrysanthemums, were arranged at intervals along the corridors which led off from the central reception area.

'I have an appointment to see Sister Boon.'

'Oh, yes. Along the corridor to your right, and through the swing doors.'

She walked slowly, savouring the atmosphere of svelte luxury. A velvet voice reached her along the corridor. 'It can't really be you, Emily!'

She had passed the half-open door, marked 'Consulting Room', and was aware that there was someone inside. Now Andrew Dashwood had come out into the corridor, and was following her. She stopped, the colour coming into her cheeks in spite of her wish to remain cool and collected. 'Good morning, Doctor.'

'What on earth are you doing here?'

'I work here. At least, I start tomorrow.'

He smiled, and his blue eyes lit up. 'And there was I thinking I'd made no impression on you.'

'I applied for the job two months ago.'

'Now there's a coincidence.' He was still smiling, and she was painfully aware of the force of his charm. 'It would be even more of a coincidence if you were coming to my department.'

'I'm in neurology.'

'Ah, pity. I'm no neurologist. I'm senior physician here.'

She couldn't help saying, 'You're young to be a senior.'

'I'm older than I look, Emily.'

Yes, there was maturity in his eyes, and an air of quiet confidence that spoke of years of experience. She said, feeling less shy with him, 'Last time we spoke you made it fairly clear that you wanted nothing to do with me or my fiancé.'

'Ah, the Honourable Gerald. I recall leaving in some dismay. Sorry, Emily, but he has that effect on me sometimes. I didn't mean anything personal towards you.'

'You are business partners, though? In SEAH?'

'Oh, yes, myself and several others.' Dr Dashwood indicated his room. 'Can I offer you coffee?'

'No, thank you. I'm seeing Sister Boon at eleven.' Emily was a trifle disappointed. She would have liked the chance to get to know Dashwood's side of the argument over a cup of coffee. 'I must hurry.'

'Maybe we could do lunch? My room at twelve?'

'Perhaps.' She wasn't sure if she liked his confident approach. He knew she was engaged, yet he was free with his invitation.

'Good. Till then.' He nodded and went back to his room, and Emily walked on, feeling as though she had betrayed Gerald by making this tryst with another man. She had to remind herself that Andrew Dashwood was now a colleague, and lunching with colleagues went on all the time with no evil intent.

Sister Marilyn Boon was not what Emily had expected from her cheerful voice. She was thin and rather bony, and her middle-aged Chinese face was almost hidden by large tinted glasses perched on a tiny nose. But the cheerfulness was still there, and the welcome was genuine. 'It's a six-month contract with the option of renewal. Is that what we agreed?'

'Yes.'

'And the pay? Was anything mentioned?'

'Just usual rates.'

'That is the policy. But there is overtime, and the

management policy is to pay nurses bonuses for outstanding work, so the standard of care is high here.'

Emily tried not to be too delighted at the generous salary. 'And accommodation? I'm afraid I haven't found anywhere to live.'

'Oh, we can easily find you a room in the nurses' home. It's that wooden building across the quadrangle.'

For a moment it sounded like a shed, but as soon as Emily saw the smart louvred bungalow, set among travellers' palm trees, she knew she had found a home from home. She was soon settled in her own room with bath and telephone, and had rung the Tanglin to send her belongings. Then she telephoned Gerald's apartment. The phone rang a few times, before a woman's fruity voice answered. 'Hello? The Honourable Mr Montague's residence?'

'It's Emily Fairlie here.'

'Oh, Emily, I'm Annabel! So nice to talk to you. I'm sure Gerald will have told you about me. He isn't here just now — gone to the office, I think, but stopping off at the bank first. Would you like to come round? I'm dying to meet you.' She sounded gushing, but artificial.

Emily had planned to stay at the hospital all day. 'Maybe you could write down my address for him, Annabel? I'll be staying at the Bungalow Hari Raya. It's just off Edinburgh Place.'

'It sounds a stylish address for a —' Annabel was clearly going to be patronising, but pulled herself up in time. 'A very prestigious part of the city, Emily. I'll pass him the message.'

'I'll be here all day. If I'm going out, I'll let him know. Bye, Annabel.'

'Bye, Emily. Dying to meet you.' Emily put the receiver down thoughtfully. Annabel? A Girl Friday, maybe? Or was she perhaps one of those budding

Madam Butterflies Gerald mentioned? He thought a lot of her taste, if he wanted her to show Emily what to buy in Singapore. Did she live in his apartment block? She must feel a bit pushed out by Emily's arrival, if she had been with him for long. No wonder she watched her language, and gushed a bit too much. She knew she must stay on the right side of Gerald's fiancée, or else.

It might have been helpful to get to know Annabel. But it was too late now. Emily looked at her watch. She would keep that lunch date with Andrew Dashwood—but only, she told herself, to find out just where he and Gerald disagreed so violently. Surely, as a friend of both men, she might be able to do some mediation and bring them together again. She tried on her new uniform, a fitted white cotton dress, then hung it up in the wardrobe, and tidied her hair. She just had time to meet her chief, the neurosurgeon, Dr Mehtani, in the neurology ward, and find out what her nursing colleagues were like. Emily walked out into the heat of the day, and crossed the lawns in the shade of the travellers' palms. The air was kind on her skin, and birds sang in the bushes. Life seemed good, and Emily was optimistic as she entered the hospital and found the neurology department.

The other sister, Sue Brown, was Australian and quite pretty in a short-haired, efficient sort of way. Her manner was restrained, though, and, although she welcomed Emily, her voice didn't match the words. 'I hope you'll get along here, Emily. You have very good references.'

'I'm looking forward to it. When would you like me to start.'

'Here's the timetable.'

'Oh, but——' There didn't seem much time off.

'Anything wrong?'

'I understood I would be part-time.'

'That's correct, Emily, but we have two girls off on vacation, and you have to fill in for them.'

'I see.' Emily studied the paper. She didn't mind hard work, but Gerald wouldn't be too pleased.

Sister Brown went back to her office. A Chinese staff nurse had been quietly putting some files away, and now she said, 'I'm Mai Li. Welcome to the Ambassador.' There was a definite twinkle in her eye. 'Don't mind Sister—she's going out with Dr Dashwood, and everybody has heard that a glamorous new nurse came to his assistance when Mr Mahmoud collapsed in the Tanglin Palace. She had it in for you before you even arrived, Emily. But don't let it bother you. It's easy to keep your head down, and the Mahmoud affair will soon blow over.'

'Glamorous? Me?' Emily grinned. 'She'll soon find out I'm no threat.'

'Want to come to lunch in the staff dining-room?'

'Lunch? Oh, I've already arranged to meet someone.'

'Who?'

Emily felt guilty suddenly. 'Mai Li, is Sister Brown very serious about Dr Dashwood?'

'Crazy about him. Isn't everyone? He's gorgeous.' Mai Li looked hard at Emily. 'Don't tell me—you're meeting Dashwood. Well, if you value your eyesight, I'd call it off if I were you.'

Emily took a deep breath. Any trouble here was not of her making, but she knew very well that to go ahead and meet Andrew Dashwood was not a good idea. 'Actually, I've just remembered—I am free, after all. Shall we go?'

'Great. Won't be a moment putting these away. I'll just check that the next shift have arrived.' And within moments Emily was being taken to the luxury restaurant that went by the modest name of staff dining-room. 'Like it?' Mai Li gestured towards the gleaming white tables and the well-stocked buffet. 'It's mainly Singaporean food, but you'll find fish and European roast meat if you look carefully. Chopsticks optional.'

Emily chose the fish, and a glass of mineral water, and the two nurses found a corner seat where they were slightly shielded from the other tables by a potted palm. Slowly she began to find out about the department as they ate. 'Well, it looks as though I'll get on fine here as long as I don't run into Dr Dashwood again.'

'Was it really him you had a date with?'

'It wasn't a date. I only wanted to talk about the South East Asia Health Club. My fiancé is a fellow board member. But it can wait. It isn't important.'

'You're engaged? That's good. Then Sue can't be jealous of you.'

Emily picked up a flake of fish with her fork. 'Yes, that's it — I'm engaged.' But somehow she felt that this situation wasn't quite right. If she wanted to settle down properly in neuro, then she really ought to be properly engaged. It was something she would have to speak to Gerald about next time she saw him. She didn't want to be Gerald's property. Uneasily she knew that at the moment she didn't want any intimacy between them. But if she wanted life to go smoothly, she must make the decision very soon. It would calm Gerald, and it would satisfy Sister Brown.

And then a dark male voice interrupted the two nurses' conversation. 'I waited for you, Emily.'

She looked up. Dashwood's face was impassive. Emily didn't want to make things more complex, so she merely apologised. 'I didn't realise it was a definite arrangement. So sorry.'

'It's quite all right.' Andrew Dashwood was elegant,

cool and dismissive. Emily felt ashamed for not letting him know. But she knew that from now on it didn't make sense to show Sue Brown — or anyone else — that since the Mahmoud episode Emily and Dashwood were sort of friends. She turned back to her cooling lunch and pretended to enjoy it.

Mai Li took her to meet Dr Mehtani. Thank goodness here was a sensible and uncomplicated man, dedicated to his work, and with a no-nonsense approach to his staff. Dark-skinned and slim, he smiled, shook her hand and explained simply, 'Patients come first, Sister Fairlie. I'm aware that nurses also have their problems, but we aren't here for the nurses' good, but for the good of the patients, and if you observe that golden rule I will be a happy man.'

'That suits me very well, sir.'

Mehtani looked at the clock on the wall. 'I'm due at a clinic. I'm sure you'll soon fit in very well, won't she, Sister Brown?'

Sue Brown was standing in the doorway. It was hard to tell what she was thinking, but her voice was marginally less icy than when they first met. Mai Li must have told her about Emily's engagement. 'I'm sure she will.'

Emily found herself walking along the corridor with Sister Brown. 'So I'll start at nine tomorrow.'

'Good.' They walked without speaking. Then Sue said, 'You do know Dr Dashwood socially?'

'Not really. He knows my fiancé.'

'I see.' It was the nearest thing to a smile Emily had seen on Sue's face. She reflected sadly how cruel love could be. Sue was crazy about Dashwood. Yet it was obvious even so early in their relationship that Dashwood wasn't crazy about Sue Brown. Relationships were dangerous things.

And then the afternoon was at an end, and Emily

had heard nothing from Gerald. She wondered whether to telephone the apartment again, but didn't really want to speak to the utterly artificial Annabel. She rearranged her dresses and put away her lingerie. She showered in the tiled bathroom, and dressed in a simple cotton skirt and top. She looked at herself in the mirror. She really must get some more sophisticated clothes if she were to fit in here.

At last someone rang her doorbell. She went to open it—only to see Chang, the chauffeur, his white Mercedes parked on the road outside. 'Mr Montague sent me to bring you, madam.'

'Where are we going?'

'To his apartment, madam.'

'I'll just be five minutes, Chang.'

'Yes, madam.'

She looked through her clothes, and settled on a white raw silk suit and white sandals. She brushed her hair till it shone, remembering how Gerald loved it loose. Then she put the door key in her purse and went out, closing the door gently on her new and exciting little residence.

'Meeting Gerald?' She looked up at the voice. Dashwood had cleverly chosen the place to accost her, hidden as it was from both the bungalow and the road by a swath of hibiscus bushes. 'I'm sorry we couldn't talk earlier.'

Emily looked up at him. She was sorry too, but she wasn't going to admit it. 'I'm working for a certain Sister Brown, Dr Dashwood. And I think she's expecting you.' Emily didn't realise how reluctant she was to say that, and how much she envied Sue Brown when the young doctor swung on his heel.

She couldn't let him go so coldly. 'Goodnight,' she said, hesitantly.

IN THE HEAT OF THE SUN

He paused very briefly. 'Montague really is a prat! I wouldn't have sent my chauffeur if I were meeting someone as beautiful as you.' And he turned and merged quietly into the dusk of the sweet-scented gardens.

CHAPTER THREE

AN AMBULANCE was pulling up as Emily came out of the residence to go to Gerald's limousine. She paused to see if any help was needed, but two nurses were waiting with plasma and dressings. 'A road accident,' explained one nurse when she saw Emily staring. 'We've got Theatre on standby.'

The other nurse said, 'You're off duty, aren't you? Get a break while you can. They work you hard in this place!'

'I don't mind work,' smiled Emily. The patient appeared conscious and not too badly hurt. Emily watched as the stretcher was wheeled indoors, and felt the familiar pull of duty. True, the surroundings here were lush and beautiful. But the face of pain was always the same, and the need for kind and efficient nursing. It was with an effort that Emily turned her attention away from the clinic and towards the chauffeur Chang, standing patiently by the white Mercedes.

Gerald's apartment was in a tall circular building in the very centre of Singapore. The chauffeur was helpful, as Emily gazed up at the subtle lighting, the overflowing window-boxes, and the starry sky beyond. Even now the heat was oppressive. Chang was saying, 'All apartments here cost more than a million dollars. Very prestigious place to have an address.'

Emily smiled to herself. 'I am impressed, Chang, honestly. Since I arrived I have seen nothing but luxury, class, good taste, and a love of excellence. I knew Gerald would fit into this set-up easily.'

'Oh, yes, lah. Honourable Gerald very favoured member of society. Very important man in SEAH.'

He locked the Mercedes, and led her up to the main door. An armed guard in a flamboyant uniform looked carefully at Chang's pass—even though he clearly knew him very well—before bowing to Emily and allowing them to enter the airy foyer, and pressing the button for one of the lifts.

'My darling!' But Gerald had sprung away from a buxom blonde woman as Emily entered, and his face was flushed. 'Welcome to your future home.'

'Hello, Gerald.' Emily tried not to imagine why they had moved apart so guiltily.

Gerald had regained his good humour. 'This is Annabel Gray—my PA.'

Annabel stood up. She was wearing a black suit, with a very short skirt, the lapels of the jacket studded with sequins. She said with a friendly smile, 'We've spoken on the phone. How are you, Emily?'

Emily shook her hand, noting that the blonde hair was a touch darker at the roots. Did Annabel go blonde because Gerald was turned on by fair hair? They all stood for a moment, the atmosphere awkward, until the manservant came in noiselessly, carrying a tray of full glasses of champagne. Emily found herself thinking of the accident patient who had been wheeled in ten minutes ago. Her thoughts drifted to the neuro ward in the Ambassador Clinic, and the cases Mai Li had told her were to be admitted tomorrow. She wished she had stayed in the residence tonight, and prepared herself for her day's work tomorrow. She felt like an intruder into Gerald's palatial lounge. She tried to be relaxed. 'Your health clubs must be doing well, Gerald. What a lovely apartment.'

He sipped his champagne and nodded. 'It's a good

business to be in just now, but not good enough. We ought to expand quickly, while everyone is preoccupied with their health, because tomorrow will be too late.'

Annabel said, her voice drawling and her accent affected, 'Do you really want him to talk business, Emily?'

Emily did, and she resented Annabel's insinuation that Emily was a dizzy blonde with no brains. 'Why is there a problem over expansion?'

Gerald seemed pleased to get it off his chest. 'The board has several new properties in Malaysia and Indonesia. Development into profitable clubs has already begun. But in Singapore land is like gold, and the one site we need is being sat on by Andrew Dashwood. That is the site that will make us a mint — where our returns could be highest. But only if we strike now.'

'Why won't he sell?'

'Don't ask me! Dog in a manger.'

'But he's on the board too.'

Gerald swung on his heel and went over to pour himself another drink. 'And the sooner he's off the better. They wanted a medical adviser — but he cares more about his patients than the good of the company.'

Emily could see that a medical man would naturally think of his patients first. She said, 'There must be another reason.'

Both Gerald and Annabel stared at Emily. Gerald's voice was silky. 'And why do you say that, my dear? Are you on his side?'

'I'm on no one's side. No, that's not true — I'm on your side, Gerald; but Dr Dashwood must have an excuse for not selling to you. Hasn't he given you his own views?'

'No. I blame it on personal jealousy. The man lives

in a tiny bungalow in Serangoon, Emily, and eats from the hawker stalls. He must have some money, but never has any available. It sounds crazy to me. Maybe he keeps too many mistresses... Now a consultant who lives like that must be envious of my personal success, and want to stop me doing well.'

Annabel saw Emily wasn't convinced. Dashwood did not appear to be a jealous man to Emily. Annabel said, 'That's very true, Emily. He's a very secretive man — very quiet. There's a lot he doesn't say about himself. Don't trust him, Emily, dear. What sane colleague would do what he is doing when it's for the general good of the company profits?'

Emily had her own ideas about Andrew Dashwood, and her first impressions had been favourable. But she had to admit she didn't know him very well. 'Yes, I see what you mean.'

Annabel took this to indicate that Emily was now on Gerald's side, and her manner relaxed. 'Let's send for some dinner, Gerry.'

Emily raised an eyebrow. Was it really usual for a couple who were almost engaged to share their first night's dinner with another woman? She wasn't the jealous type, but she did say casually, 'You live near by, Annabel?'

There was an imperceptible silence before Annabel said hurriedly, 'Oh, yes, only a stone's throw round the corner.'

Gerald saw what Emily meant. 'Annabel, could you look out the papers on the Haw Sing project, please? I'm sure Emily would like to see just what we could do if Andrew Dashwood got off his backside and co-operated.'

'Oh, yes, I would, please.'

Annabel looked at them both before leaving the

room. Gerald reached out and took Emily in his arms. 'I'm sorry, my darling. Annabel has been doing a lot of overtime for me on this project, and she has only just finished a pile of word processing. I know I should send her home, but — well —'

Emily had no choice but to take it coolly. She smiled casually, and disentangled herself from Gerald's embrace. She walked to the window, and looked down over the breathtaking expanse of brilliant lights and neon signs, lighting up lush palm trees, floodlit swimming-pools and elegant gardens among the skyscrapers. 'On no account must you send her home, Gerald. I'm the intruder — the newcomer, and I don't want to upset your routine in any way. I'm sure in time she'll see that we need time alone together. But not tonight, not on my account.'

'That's very sweet and reasonable of you.' Gerald seemed unsure of her calm acceptance of having his secretary to dinner. He looked hard at her, but Emily gazed innocently out of the window, fascinated by what she saw. Satisfied, Gerald called the butler. 'The restaurant can deliver now, Lee.'

'Yes, sir.'

Over a delicious Chinese meal, eaten at Gerald's expensive mahogany carved table, Annabel told Emily what a superb health club they had planned and had designed for this site of Dashwood's. Over coffee they spread the designs over the thick Indian carpet and explained with pride that nothing was to be omitted for complete inner and outer health. 'The Haw Sing Centre is going to be the best in South East Asia — as soon as we get the site. We want it to be a place every visiting businessman feels he must see while in Singapore. A bit like the Tana Merah Golf Club — a status symbol for anyone who is anyone.'

Emily expressed her admiration. 'It certainly doesn't make sense to refuse to sell the land. I'm sure Dr Dashwood will get a good price for it. It does sound as though he's holding out for some reason. You have offered him a good price?'

'The best. The trouble is, as I told you, Singapore land is very precious.'

'No alternative sites?'

'No. We must have a city centre property to appeal to the high-spending business clientele. There's nothing else available in the city.'

'What is the building being used for now?'

Gerald shrugged. 'There are shops on the ground floor, and upstairs is some sort of overspill for his Ambassador activities. He insists there's nowhere else for them to move to.'

Annabel said sharply, 'You're going to work at the Ambassador, Emily. You might be able to help us out—put the case of the health club, that sort of thing, if you come across Dashwood.'

'He's not in my department, but if I get the chance, then certainly I'll push your side of the argument.' And Emily meant it. The plans for the health club were truly splendid. There seemed no reason for Dr Dashwood to refuse to allow it to be built.

Chang drove Emily back to the Bungalow Hari Raya at midnight. As she thanked him and walked up to her own neat front door, she smiled at what Dashwood had said earlier—'I wouldn't have sent my chauffeur if I were meeting someone as beautiful as you.' Emily consoled herself with the thought that they had discussed their relationship and agreed not to rush things. She couldn't blame Gerald for holding back—after all, it was what she had asked for. But did Annabel Gray have to behave as though she owned that apartment?

Emily undressed, and laid out her smart white uniform dress for the morning. She was sitting, dressed only in a skimpy nightie, brushing her long fair hair in front of the dressing-table mirror, when she heard voices outside. Peeping through the Venetian blinds, she saw two figures she recognised by the light over the residence door — Sue Brown and Andrew Dashwood. He was still wearing his white coat, which hung open over a crumpled shirt and loosened tie. His hair was dishevelled, and his handsome eyes were shadowed. Their voices were low, but she caught a few words. 'I want to be told about that patient first thing, Sue.'

'Don't worry. You can trust me.'

'I know, honey. And thanks for tonight.'

'Any time, Andrew.' Sue reached up and kissed his cheek. Emily held her breath and hoped they didn't look up and notice the displacement of the Venetian blind. Sue turned away and let herself into her own flat. Andrew stood for a moment until her door had closed. Then he turned to go. But first he paused, then looked directly at Emily's window. She froze, unable to let the blind drop, yet scarlet with embarrassment at being caught in the act of spying on him. For a moment no one moved, and the screeching of the insects in the grass sounded like a great chorus of accusation. Then Dashwood looked down, a smile playing at the corner of his mouth, and walked slowly out of the circle of light, casually back towards the hospital.

Emily felt as though he was laughing at her, and at Gerald. He must be enjoying having this power over him. Yes, Annabel was probably right — he was envious of Gerald's money and success. She already knew there was genuine personal enmity between the two men.

Otherwise why hold out over a piece of real estate that could net him millions? No, they genuinely hated each other. Emily replaced the blind, and walked over to the bed thoughtfully. She would try hard to persuade Dashwood to sell that site. It was the least she could do for her fiancé.

Sister Sue Brown was on duty before Emily made it to the ward next morning, and looked pointedly at her watch. Emily made no excuses, but calmly got on with the ward work she was set, going round first to do temperatures and blood-pressures. There was no point in starting an argument. Sue was her superior, and it was wise to keep her head down.

It was a post-operative ward, but there were also some non-surgical cases, and also patients waiting for tests such as angiograms and CT scans. Almost all patients were in single rooms, but their doors were kept open, and some of the children were two to a room. That made sense, as children were easily frightened or bored in hospital, even with the fatherly Dr Mehtani in charge. Emily lost no time in getting to know little Amy Lau, who was having the valve inside her head changed for a larger one, to deal with her hydrocephalus. A cheery little mite with twinkling black eyes, Amy proudly told Emily that she had already had two operations like this. 'And I will need one more. But when I am big there is no need to change the valve because I will not change in size any more!'

Emily asked Mai Li during their morning break about the accident victim of the previous night. 'Did they have to operate?'

'Yes, there was a ruptured spleen. But the patient was also already on warfarin for a deep vein thrombosis, so Dr Dashwood had to stay with her until the bleeding had stopped, and adjust her heparin. Sue stayed on duty to help him. The patient will be fine as long as the bleeding stays under control.'

'So that's why he was still in his white coat at midnight.'

'What was that?' Sister Sue Brown had appeared apparently super-sensitive to the name Dashwood. 'Shouldn't you two nurses be back at work?'

Mai Li looked at the clock, which showed plainly that they had another five minutes' break. But Emily rose from her seat, unwilling to be the cause of any problems in the ward, and made her way back to work. She had nothing against Sue Brown, but Sue would go on being suspicious until Emily had proved that there was nothing between Andrew Dashwood and herself. She would have to be careful. She knew just how acid Sue could be. And Sue had no need to be jealous — none at all. Emily had an understanding with Gerald Montague, and in spite of a few misgivings at the beginning she would keep her word to him, and stand up for him against Andrew Dashwood any time she believed Gerald to be in the right.

'Nurse!' A child's voice, agonisingly shrill. Emily ran to the room. A worried Chinese boy was standing at the foot of his cot, calling her, gripping the end of the cot. Lennie was handsome, but totally bald. In the opposite cot, a smaller boy was thrashing his limbs in an attack of grand mal. Emily coolly made sure Kim wasn't biting his tongue, and lifted Lennie on to her lap, soothing him while she also gently wiped Kim's face with a tissue as his fit subsided. 'It's all right, Lennie. Your friend Kim is all right.'

'But he made funny noises.'

'Yes, that's quite usual.' Her calm voice and her comforting arm quickly made the child feel secure again. Emily explained as simply as she could, 'That's why he is in hospital, Lennie. The doctor is going to make him well with an operation, so that he won't have these little attacks any more. See? His eyes are opening. Now he will be drowsy for a little while, but he'll soon be ready to play with you again.'

'I had an operation. Is it like mine? Inside his head?'

'Yes, that's right.'

'So they will shave off his hair too?'

'Yes, Lennie, they will. But it will soon grow strong and black again.'

The child responded more to the gentle reassurance in her voice than the meaning of the words. And as Kim came round, and lay for a few moments gathering his thoughts, none the worse for his experience, Lennie's brow cleared, and he called to him, 'Hey, when you ready to play with me again?' and the boys were soon laughing.

'Well done, Emily.' It was Dr Dashwood's voice, and for a moment she forgot she was supposed to be his enemy and welcomed him with a smile. 'That was a tactful and very correct lesson in how to handle children. Have you worked with them before?'

'As a matter of fact, quite a lot.' She thought back to her time at the Royal Lester. It seemed to be millions of miles away, not just eight thousand. She said sadly, 'It always seems so much more cruel, when a child has a problem. They are so innocent in their suffering. At least adults can cope with illness. It seems so unfair that children have to suffer so much.'

Andrew Dashwood came into the room, and smiled at the two boys, as he said to Emily, 'It's the trust in their eyes, isn't it? They trust us so totally, and you and I know that we can't always cure them. It's heartbreaking.'

Emily looked up at the lean, tanned face, the square

jaw and the perfect profile, and felt a new affinity with this handsome young doctor. She knew there were many good doctors, but not many who openly admitted to not being God. He turned suddenly and caught the look in her eyes. Dashwood smiled at her, as though reading her thoughts, and Emily hastily said the first thing that came into her head. 'We can only do our best.' Then she said, 'That's a trite thing to say, but I think you know what I mean.'

Lennie had fallen asleep, and Dashwood lifted little Kim on to his knee, as he said quietly to Emily, 'I know exactly what you mean, and it isn't trite at all. I've gone to sleep many a night wishing with all my heart that I could do more for a little child—work some miracle.' She saw something raw and hurting in his gentle blue eyes, and the depth of pain was suddenly rather frightening, so that Emily dared not prolong the conversation. Kim sat quietly, his head tilted to look up at the doctor, recognising the sincerity and comfort in his voice. Emily backed away, feeling that at this moment neither boy nor doctor needed her.

'There was no need to go into that room, Nurse!' Sister Brown had just noticed Dashwood, and her brow darkened as she recognised Emily stealing away.

'The child had a fit, Sister.'

'Oh. Did you enter it on his chart?' Her voice was still sharp.

'No—I'll go and do it now.'

'I'll do it.' Sister Brown looked more cheerful, now that she had a chance of seeing her beloved Dr Dashwood. 'Was it a grand mal again?'

'Yes.'

'All right, I'll do his chart. Run along now. You're needed in the women's wing.'

'Yes, Sister.' Emily was better qualified than this

testy young woman to run a ward like this, but she accepted her orders gracefully, and walked quietly away.

Later Emily was sitting over a plate of noodles when Mai Li came over to join her. 'Are you free this evening, Emily?'

'I'm working from six till nine.'

'But that's far too many hours.'

'Sister Brown tells me it's my duty to fill in for anyone who's off sick.'

'It's against the rules to work such long hours.'

Emily smiled as her young friend began getting heated. 'Don't worry, Mai Li. I didn't work very strenuously today. And I do have an hour off for dinner.'

'All the same, I think I know why she's doing this to you.' Mai Li wielded her chopsticks dexterously, conveying fried rice from plate to mouth with quite amazing speed, yet still managing to look dainty. She said between mouthfuls, 'You would not be treated like this in London.'

'In London I was sister. I was in charge.'

'I bet you wish you had stayed there. What made you come to Singapore, Emily?'

'My fiancé works here,' said Emily rather lamely. 'I thought I'd like to experience his adopted country for myself.'

'And now?'

'One cross sister isn't the end. And I love working with the kids. I think I'll stick it out for a while.'

'At least you have your wedding to look forward to.'

'Wedding! Yes—oh, yes, of course I have.' But Emily somehow could not conjure up a mental picture of herself in white, standing demurely next to Gerald, turning into Mrs St Clair Montague. Somehow the picture also contained a handsome rounded young woman with dyed blonde hair and a black sequinned suit. . . 'My PA,' Gerald had called her, but perhaps on Annabel's side there was more to it than that.

Back in the women's wing, Emily found that she and another nurse were expected to look after all the patients in the block, medical and surgical. The other nurse explained that evening duties were quite hard. 'But at least we get paid a little more. The supper trays need clearing. I'll take the ones on the left — you do the right.'

'Sure.' It was an opportunity to get to know the patients, and Emily introduced herself to a variety of ladies, with problems varying from appendicitis to leg ulcers. But the hours were beginning to tell, and by the time nine o'clock came round her eyes were starting to close.

Night Sister sent her packing, with profuse thanks for working so conscientiously. Emily accepted her thanks with a wry smile, wishing Night Sister could exchange jobs with Susan Brown. 'Goodnight, Sister.' Emily walked out into the warm bath of Singapore air, and paused for a moment to steady herself. It had been a long day, and her head felt light.

She began to walk slowly along the little path that led through the gardens to the nurses' bungalows. The stars and the city lights began to swim before her eyes, and she was glad there were wooden benches along the walkway. The scent of frangipani and jasmine was sweet, almost cloying, in the moonlight, and Emily reached for the arm of a bench, and sat down for a moment, bending her head down between her knees.

As she sat, doubled up, she could hear the gentle notes of a piano coming from an open window. Gradually its clarity and beauty caught her attention, and she sat up slowly, her hair fallen out of its restraining clips now and tangled round her shoulders as she listened to Mozart and gazed up at the stars.

She hardly heard the footsteps on the paved path, but she was vaguely aware that someone was coming through the palm trees, and that suddenly a pair of white-trousered legs was standing in front of her. She looked up, first at the long, muscular legs under the thin cloth, then at the slim body in a dark green T-shirt that broadened into square, athletic shoulders, topped by the boyish yet weary face of Andrew Dashwood. She stared for a moment, and then said the first thing that came into her head. 'What are you doing here?'

He smiled slightly. 'I work here. I'm going home.' But his face changed as he saw she was still in uniform. 'Emily, you haven't worked a twelve-hour shift on your first day!'

'Something like that.'

'What time are you in tomorrow?'

'Nine.'

He sat down beside her, his long legs akimbo, and leaned forward to look at her, his blue eyes concerned. 'Why didn't you complain?'

'I was told it was usual procedure.'

'It isn't. Especially in this heat when you aren't acclimatised. I'd better get you home to bed. Plenty of fluids, Emily, and a good rest. I'll let Sue know you won't be in tomorrow.'

'But I might feel fine tomorrow.'

'You're suffering from heat exhaustion. You need at least twenty-four hours' rest, and then you must start on short shifts.'

'Andrew——' She didn't realise she was using his first name. 'Please don't interfere. You only saw me by chance. Leave me to work things out for myself.' She didn't say that Sue Brown would make her life much more of a misery if Andrew Dashwood showed he was concerned about Emily.

'All right — I won't say a word — if you come along with me now.'

She stood up, still feeling light-headed, and was propped up comfortingly by Andrew's strong arm. He took the key from her fingers and unlocked her door, and soon had her lying on the bed. He brought her a glass of water, and stood beside her as she drank. Then he rifled in the cupboard and found some clear soup, which he warmed in a small pan. After she had drunk it, he insisted that she undress and put on her nightdress. Too tired to care how skimpy it was, she obeyed him, and lay back against the pillows. He brought her a jug and glass beside the bed, and next time she opened her eyes he told her gently to drink it all before morning.

'Boyfriend too busy making money to meet you after your first day's work?' he asked quietly.

'I asked him not to. I asked him for — my own space.' She was too tired to argue with Andrew, but she noticed his personal dislike of Gerald creeping into his voice. Weakly she tried to stick up for him. 'He would have come if I wanted it. You mustn't let your own animosity colour your opinions about him.'

'My animosity! What about his?' But Andrew restrained himself quickly. 'Forget I said that. Lie back. I'll leave you to sleep now, and let's just hope you are well in the morning. My medical opinion is that you ought to rest tomorrow.'

'I won't be silly, I promise. Just don't — don't go to Sue on my behalf.'

Andrew smiled. 'I see. All right, I promise.'

Emily leaned back, satisfied. She thought Andrew

must have gone, but then she sensed something warm close to her cheek, and his face touched her as his lips sought hers. 'Goodnight, Emily.' It was meant to be a brief kiss, but somehow he didn't draw back. Within moments his arms had drawn her gently from the pillow into his arms, and they were embracing with a languid yet passionate intensity. She knew she had wanted this, knew how attracted she had been to the handsome young doctor the very first time she saw him.

But she pushed him away then, with all the strength she had left. 'How despicable, to take advantage of a girl's weakness.'

Andrew was already striding to the door. 'You're right, of course. It won't happen again. I don't know what came over me.' He paused and looked back at Emily, who had fallen back on the pillows, her hair spread out and tangled, her heart thumping with more than just a little heat exhaustion. . . 'I hope I don't see you in the ward tomorrow. It would be medically very silly.' And he closed the door gently behind him. Emily closed her eyes, finding, to her consternation, tears squeezing between her lashes and rolling down her cheeks. Never in her whole twenty-four years had any kiss ever been so sweet and so desirable. And this man was an enemy, according to Gerald. He was a man she must not love.

CHAPTER FOUR

IN THE brightness of a new morning, Emily felt as optimistic as the day. How could anyone from a cool country fail to be delighted and beguiled by the warmth of the atmosphere, the shrill chirruping of the Indian sparrows and the hummingbirds? The palm trees outside the window cast deep shadows on the trim grass, and the scarlet hibiscus flowers opened like lovers to the sun's rays and the probing of the buzzing insects.

Emily dressed and breakfasted on juice, coffee and a ripe papaya, the fruit thoughtfully provided by Mai Li, who called early to see how she was. 'You are looking better, Emily, but maybe it be good that you have morning off.'

'I would rather come to work. What else will I do with myself all day? I'll stop work if I feel dizzy again, but honestly, Mai Li, I'm usually a fit individual.'

'You're not scared of Sue, are you?' Mai Li looked with admiration at her new friend.

Emily shook her head. Sue Brown was a prickly person, but Emily could live with that. After all, Gerald was her main reason for being here, and what happened at the clinic was only part of her part-time job. 'Not scared at all. Why should I be? I've done nothing wrong. I just feel embarrassed because she thinks I'm trying to take Andrew — er — Dr Dashwood away from her. She has the wrong idea altogether, and she is only making things unhappy for herself, not for me.'

Mai Li lifted the sculpted eyebrows over her almond eyes and shook her hair back from her porcelain cheeks. 'All right—if you say so. Then we go in together, but I keep an eye on you!'

'Thank you, Mai Li. Appreciate it. I do really like it here, you know—if only Sue could take a night job!'

Mai Li laughed. 'No way she would do that. Not if Dr Dashwood is on days! I am surprised that he does not tell her to stop chasing him.'

'Then he must like her, Mai Li, and that's his own business.' Was it? She put her hand up to her cheek, remembering how warm and strong he felt beside her, the smoothness of his skin slightly roughened, more than seventeen hours since his last shave, but the softness of his mouth, luscious and desirable over hers. She felt a throb in her temple as she recalled him, and brushed her hand over her brow.

Mai Li was quick to spot it. 'Now! You see! You are not well.'

'I'm very well!' Staunchly Emily stood up and straightened her shoulders. 'Come on, we'll be late for the Sergeant Major!'

Giggling, they made their way across the smooth lawn and along the little winding path through the palm trees and the hibiscus. Sue was indeed waiting for them, but there was a worried look on her face, and she forgot to look at her watch. She wasted no time in greetings. 'Oh, Mai Li, you haven't been in contact with Sister Boon, have you?'

'No, Sister. I haven't spoken to her for over a week.'

'Thank God! You, Nurse Fairlie?'

Emily shook her head. 'I met her on my first day, but very briefly.'

'Hallelujah. Thank goodness. I'm afraid there is a dreadful problem. Please understand, things are very serious. She is in isolation—a very high temperature and breathing problems—she is on a respirator in the

ICU, fighting for her life. Dr Dashwood is doing all he can, but so far the hospital can't find out the source of the infection. There is strict barrier nursing, of course, but we are extremely worried about the children in this ward. I'm afraid you two and I myself must do all the nursing on this ward. All the rest of the staff are contacts of Sister Boon, and they have been isolated until the virus can be found.' She looked at Emily with something of remorse. 'If only you hadn't done a twelve-hour day yesterday, Nurse Fairlie. I'm sorry about that, but it is likely you may have to do the same today, although I'll do my best to give you adequate rest.'

The two nurses stood for a moment in silence, as they took in the gravity of the situation. Then Mai Li said stoutly, 'Emily was ill last night, Sister. Should not Dr Dashwood or Dr Mehtani check her out, and make sure she isn't sickening for this mystery virus?'

Emily replied quickly, 'Don't worry about me, Sister — I only had a mild case of heat exhaustion yesterday. My symptoms are nothing like a viral problem, and I feel fine today.'

Sue looked very worried. 'All the same, better stay away from patients until you've seen one of the doctors. Go into the end room, and I'll get you checked on as soon as I can. Now, Mai Li, we'd better start with the children. I'll cut out as many unnecessary tasks as I can. The flowers can wait for the domestics, and the patients don't need to be dressed if they don't want to.'

'Yes, Sister. And naturally we must be extra careful about sterile conditions. It would be a tragedy if any of our little neuro patients ended up with a killer bug on top of the trouble they already have.'

'Yes. That's exactly the point.' Sue Brown suddenly looked very vulnerable and human, her brow furrowed in anxiety, and her fair hair straggling from her cap. Emily understood the responsibilities of a sister, and knew what must be going on in Sue's mind. Sue said, 'Come along and get started, Mai Li. Emily, you have to be patient—I'll get a doctor to you as soon as I can get someone to answer his bleep. I need you the moment you are cleared for work, understand?'

Emily said to Sue's retreating back, 'I'll be there as soon as I can. We had a situation like this in the Royal Lester—in London. It's no use panicking—we have to stay calm and wait for the lab reports. It could take days to find the organism.'

Sue turned round, and her eyes suddenly sparked with anger. 'I do realise that! I don't need your clever-clever London attitudes here! You still have to learn, Nurse Fairlie, that this is the twentieth century. The East is just as sophisticated as the West!' She swept out, leaving Emily definitely told off, to cool her heels in the spare ward at the end of the corridor.

But apparently Andrew Dashwood had overheard the conversation. As Emily sat quietly waiting for her medical examination, and trying to forgive Sue Brown for her unfortunate rudeness of manner, he tapped on the open door to attract her attention, and said, 'Sorry about the infection problem, Emily, but even sorrier at the way you're being treated.'

His blue eyes shone with sincerity, and his sudden presence brought a flush to Emily's cheeks. She had to remember that in spite of his obvious charm he was Gerald's enemy. She managed to retain her calm, and replied politely, 'These things happen.'

'You're quite philosophical. I suppose that's the only way to deal with life when it's giving you a hard time.'

Emily looked up and tried not to melt under that killingly handsome gaze. If only he didn't have such a smooth, understanding voice, and treat her with such gentle kindness. And his cheeks were smooth this morning, smelling of soap and aftershave. She took herself in hand firmly, and managed to smile at him in a casual way. 'It's the famous Kipling quote, isn't it? "If you can deal with triumph and disaster, and treat those two imposters just the same——" I've found it helps in crazy situations like this one.'

Andrew returned her smile, and sat down on the chair next to hers. He was totally self-possessed—a solid island of calm and reassurance in the situation. 'I'm glad you see things so logically, Emily. And now, if you would please take off your outer clothes and lie on the couch, it's my duty to examine you physically, and take blood for analysis. I'll do my best not to hurt you.'

His words hit her like a blow, and she felt her body grow warm with anticipation. He's going to touch me; his hands are going to move over my skin. . . She must think of Gerald, Gerald, always Gerald. And she must keep a strict hold on her reactions. She had already discovered that Andrew Dashwood wasn't easily fooled. Hadn't he noticed that she had stared at him, that first time they met in the hotel foyer? It was difficult dealing with an adversary who acted as though he had already won.

As Andrew leant over her body, stethoscope in his ears, and a detached look in his eyes, Emily stared down at the lock of his light brown hair that had fallen forward, and her flesh sparked into spasm as the hair brushed lightly against the skin of her diaphragm. He moved the stethoscope upwards, and pushed her bra aside as he listened intently to her heart and lungs. His hand was warm, and she thought he must notice the flush of excitement and embarrassment that coloured her face and neck as she looked away and tried to concentrate on the interior decoration of the little hospital room.

Andrew sat up. It was over... But he said calmly, 'And now the back, please. Sit forward, Emily. I can hear some irregularity, but I don't think it can be pathological.'

She muttered, as she pulled her bra back into position and leaned forward so that he could move the head of the stethoscope over her back and under her arms, 'I've told you, I'm fine. There's nothing wrong with me.'

Andrew didn't reply until he had finished the examination. Then he took the stethoscope from his ears and said coolly, 'No, there's nothing wrong with you except your choice of friends.'

'That was despicable!'

'True, just like your friends.' But Andrew could see that she was not going to take this lightly, and said hurriedly, 'You didn't hear that, Emily. Just letting off a bit of steam. I'm very sorry. I realise you didn't know what was going on among the board members of the Health Club Association here, and you landed in the middle of something you don't understand. Please say you forgive me.'

She replied at once, her voice cold, 'It doesn't matter what I say. You won't care whether I forgive you or not. You have your opinions and Gerald has his. You really don't give a damn what I think. I'm just an outsider.'

Andrew put his stethoscope in his pocket. His voice was impersonal. 'I have to take a sample of blood from your arm, Emily. Any preference which arm?'

'No!' She didn't know why she snapped at him.

He paused as he was taking a sterile needle from its transparent case, and his eyes bored into her. 'There isn't much point in being uppity with me, Emily. After all, I'm the only doctor who hasn't been in contact with Sister Boon.' He paused for that to sink in, and then, deftly attaching the needle to the syringe, reached out and took Emily's left arm in his gentle but strong grip. He swabbed the patch of inner elbow, and then slid the needle into the vein. Dark red blood welled into the syringe. Andrew murmured, as though just making conversation, 'We are going to be working quite closely together for the next few days.'

Icily she said, 'I had managed to work that out for myself.'

He was transferring the blood from the syringe into a sample bottle with great care. His next words threw her by their unexpected gentleness. 'Unless, of course, this sample shows something nasty. And that would upset me more than I can say.' He shook the bottle gently from side to side, to prevent clotting.

'How —— ?' Emily's throat had dried in sudden apprehension. 'How soon will you get the results?'

'I'll get the lab on to it right away. Meanwhile, I'm sure Sue can find you some paperwork to do.' He walked to the door with his usual graceful strides, turning to say, 'And that is a great pity. You're wasted on paper, when there are little patients out there who desperately need someone with your experience and your niceness.' And he was gone, the door swinging gently to.

Emily buttoned her uniform, and walked to the office to find some work she could usefully do. But her mind was on Andrew Dashwood. How could anyone be so magnetic and yet so brutal? She thought she knew the answer. He was so good-looking, so popular with women that he couldn't help but know his own attraction. If she were a man, he wouldn't speak to her like that.

But as she set to work filing some case notes from clinic, Andrew paused on his way to the ward. 'All right?'

She looked up, and the words tumbled out without her meaning them. 'From now on you speak to me as if I were a man, OK?'

For a moment he didn't answer. Then suddenly she realised he was laughing, and turned away in annoyance. She heard his words, as he leaned in the doorway before going on his way. 'Oh, Emily, Emily, I'm afraid I can't do that. Not after the last twenty minutes. You're definitely not a man, and that's an expert medical opinion!'

She heard his footsteps fading as he made his way along the corridor, and for a moment she felt again the warm, soft touch of his hand on her breast, as he held the head of the stethoscope beneath it to listen to her heart. Some irregularity, he had said. Oh, yes, he knew she was a woman, all right — and he knew the cause of that temporary irregularity of the pulse. It wasn't going to be easy working for a man who knew her so well. But he couldn't see into her mind — he couldn't know her determination to prevent any physical contact whatsoever in the future, however long they worked together.

Sue came in then. 'Nurse Fairlie, I need a list of next week's surgical cases. They will have to be contacted, to warn them that we might not be able to go ahead with their operations.'

'Yes, Sister.' Emily reached for the pile of papers. 'What about those already admitted? Will Dr Mehtani go ahead with the urgent ones?'

'He hasn't decided yet. We must get the organism

responsible for all this illness isolated. When will we know if you are clear?'

'Dr Dashwood just said as soon as possible.'

'Damn. I'll have to keep you away from patients until we know.'

'Sister, I'm certain that my illness yesterday was only through weariness and the heat. I really feel fine today. I want to get to work—I feel useless sitting in the office when there are patients to be cared for. I take it we are all wearing masks and gloves? Surely that is good enough.'

Sue looked uncertain, but she shook her head. 'No, I can't take the risk. You haven't seen Marilyn Boon—limp and unconscious, her breathing laboured and harsh. I couldn't take the responsibility for one of our little patients ending up like that. Just get out the operation lists for next week, please, and concentrate on making sure they are all contacted today.'

'Yes, Sister.'

'And Nurse Fairlie—please don't speak to Dr Dashwood—he's a very busy man and mustn't be disturbed from his work. You understand?'

'I know what you mean.' Emily eyed her superior, and then added, 'And I'm not chasing him, Sister. I'm engaged to be married to someone else. I'm not remotely interested in Andrew Dashwood as a man—he's merely a colleague. I wanted you to know that. I wanted to clear the air between us.'

Sue turned on Emily then, her anger flaring. 'Don't patronise me, Nurse Fairlie! I don't care if you're engaged or divorced—all I care about is running this ward well. So get on with your work at once.' And she swept out, her thin face red with annoyance. Emily's attempt to calm things had backfired and, sighing, she turned back to her deskwork and reached for next week's lists.

In spite of the atmosphere of anxiety and tension, there was very little for the patients to do, and the occupational therapists worked alongside Sue and Mai Li finding reading books and colouring books to pass the time between meals and TV. Emily waited tensely for the results of her blood test. Every time Andrew Dashwood passed the door of the office, she looked up hopefully, and each time he just shook his head and didn't come in.

It took three days before she was given the all-clear. Emily was sitting in her little flat, wondering when Gerald was going to get in touch, when someone knocked at the door. Hoping to find the chauffeur had come to whisk her off to Gerald's apartment, she opened the door, only to see the handsome figure of Andrew Dashwood, dressed in tailored trousers and shirt, his hair neatly waving back, and a smile on his lips. 'Thought I'd come and give you the good news myself.'

'I'm clear? No abnormality in my blood?'

'NAD, Emily. Like a drink to celebrate?'

'Oh, yes — er — no, thank you.' Emily could see that Sue Brown's car was still in the car park, and she didn't want to be seen with Andrew after her protestations about him to Sue.

'You don't need to worry about Gerald. He's away in Bangkok for a couple of days. It keeps him off my back anyway! Come on, Emily — you've been sitting in purdah for long enough.'

'I'd like to go out, Andrew — but not with you.'

'Well, I think you owe it to me. We could talk about the health clubs. My side of the story? I'm sure you have been told what a swine I am by your boyfriend.'

'Well, yes, I have actually.'

'Then you owe it to me to hear the facts.'

'I do?'

'Yes — and don't keep me here on the doorstep where everyone can see us.'

'So you are worried about Sue Brown after all.' She stepped aside, allowing him to enter, and closed the door behind him. 'I've already told her that I don't intend to trespass on her patch.'

Andrew swung round. 'Emily, I'm no one's property, you know.' His tone was one of mild reproof. 'I'm a carefree bachelor, with no commitments, no promises and no intention of being tied down in the foreseeable future.' He paused. 'And so how about that drink?'

'I'd like to get out for a while. Shall I meet you somewhere in half an hour?'

'Emily, this is silly. You don't have to slink around as though we were doing something guilty by going out together. Come along now. Let's go to the Raffles for a real Singapore Sling?'

'All right.' She wanted to. She liked Andrew's company, his conversation and his attitude to life. Also she would get the chance of trying to persuade him to sell his land to the Health Club Association. That would be a feather in her cap, if Gerald returned from Thailand to find the valuable city site offered to him. She brushed her hair back, leaving it swinging on her shoulders, and found some pretty shoes. She was wearing thin silk trousers with a batik tunic, and Andrew's look was appreciative.

They took a cab to the Raffles, its familiar white frontage and travellers' palms floodlit and very photogenic. 'We'll have a drink first, and then decide where to eat.'

'Oh, but——'

'Emily, I've worked my butt off for four days. Why not enjoy being able to relax? It doesn't happen often.'

'You're right, of course.'

'Thank you. Why are you so determined to be hard work?'

'Because I'm engaged and you—whatever you say to deny it—have some sort of commitment to Sue.'

Andrew sipped his sling and said, 'She may think so, but I've only taken her to dinner a few times. That doesn't constitute a binding engagement in my book.'

Emily smiled and decided not to argue with him any more. He was right—time was too short. 'Tell me about yourself. Where do you live?'

'I'll show you one day.' He sounded cagey all of a sudden. 'Just a small place.'

'Close by?'

'Yes, not very far.' But he didn't go into details, and Emily decided not to pry. He said, 'So you came out to marry Gerald Montague? How well did you know him?'

'I thought I knew him very well. He spent six months in London, and we had a wonderful time together, even though he ran his business by fax, and was inseparable from his cellphone. But——'

'I knew there would be a "but" in it somewhere.'

'Don't be so smug. We hit it off because he was on vacation after an op. for appendicitis, and we had lots of time to go to shows and live the good life in London—wining and dining every weekend. Of course, here he's a very busy man, and somehow—there doesn't seem so much room in his life for me except as a society hostess.'

'So that's why you took a job.'

'Yes, I think it is. I don't mind being a hostess—in fact I enjoy giving parties, but somehow it all seems so clinical now—no fun about it.'

'That's Singapore, Emily. It's a competitive society.'

'I'm beginning to see that. Is that why you are holding out over selling your property to SEAH? Are you striking your own little opposition to development?'

'Nothing so dramatic. I just think the Haw Sing Centre is better used as it is now.' His jaw set in a firm line, and his blue eyes were steely suddenly. 'The health clubs are a good idea, but it's frankly silly to believe that without a city centre site they won't do well.'

'Is it true that by selling you would become a millionaire?'

'Yes.'

'You are either very stubborn, or something of a saint.'

Andrew burst out laughing, and his face took on its more familiar relaxed look again. But she had seen the cast-iron resolve behind his affable, friendly exterior, and she knew that Andrew Dashwood was a much stronger character than she had assumed at first. He reached out a hand and put it over Emily's, squeezing hers slightly. She found herself suddenly lost for words at the unexpected tenderness of his touch. He said gently, 'You really are a very lovely woman.'

'Thank you.' Her voice was low as she met his gaze, and read real admiration in his eyes.

'I think I'll take you to the Pan Pacific for seafood. You must be hungry by now.'

'I was going to have scrambled eggs for supper.'

'Keep them for another day. We'll have lobster thermidor and a bottle of champagne.' But at that moment his pager bleeped. He detached it from his belt and switched it off. 'Damn. They need me back at the hospital.'

'It's all right. I prefer scrambled eggs anyway.'

He got to his feet. 'The lobster is only postponed. Shall I drop you at your flat?'

Emily said, making a sudden decision, 'No, I'll make my own way back, thank you. I'd like to wander around Singapore at night. It all looks so exotic and wonderfully alive.'

He put a hand on her shoulder and squeezed it gently. 'Don't stay out too late — another heavy day tomorrow.'

'I know. Thanks for the drink, Andrew.' She watched him thread his way through the well-dressed clientele, pause to speak to someone he recognised, and then he was gone, out into the tropical night.

Emily knew what she wanted to do. She intended calling at Gerald's apartment, just to see if Annabel really did stay there or not. It was time she got to the bottom of that relationship, and found out just where she stood with Gerald. As she walked out down the marble steps, a trishaw man looked expectantly at her. Smiling, she climbed into the ramshackle contraption, and was briskly pedalled round the block and up Stamford Street towards the city.

CHAPTER FIVE

WITH beating heart, Emily paused in the elegant foyer of Gerald's wealthy apartment block. Was this really the man she had met and fallen in love with? He seemed strange and far away now. She pressed his bell and waited. Gerald was in Bangkok, but perhaps the butler would be there, or the maid. After a short silence there was a sound of static as the phone was lifted in the apartment, and a woman's voice said, 'Hello, yes?'

It was Annabel. Emily forced herself to remain calm. There were lots of reasons why his secretary could still be there in the evening. 'Emily Fairlie here, Annabel.'

The languid voice changed, put on a welcoming tone that was pure artificiality. 'Why, Emily, how super. Do come up. The left-hand lift, dear.'

As the lift whooshed silently up, and the door slid back, Emily slipped off her shoes and stepped out into Gerald's opulent lounge. It was decorated in black and cream, with bowls of purple orchids strategically placed to give lavish bursts of colour. Annabel was draped over a cream satin sofa. She was wearing a loose caftan in some glittery silver material, and her feet were bare, toenails painted purple to match the orchids. There was a tall wine glass beside her on the cream Indian carpet. Emily said quietly, 'So you do live with Gerald, then. I wondered.'

Annabel's pale eyes swivelled towards her visitor, and her face became impassive. 'Oh, no, my dear. I'm only here to work while he's away. And to take calls.

It's so much easier to have someone on call who can take decisions while he is absent.'

It sounded plausible. Emily said, 'He didn't tell me he was going away.'

Annabel answered quickly, 'That's my fault. You needed space, and I thought it better that he didn't ring you. He wanted to.'

Emily gave a slight smile. 'I didn't think Gerald was the kind of man who took advice.'

'Only from me, dear—he needed someone to give him the woman's viewpoint, and I just knew you would hate to be crowded by too many telephone calls—you would think he was checking up on you.'

'I see.' Emily had to admire Annabel's ready answers.

'Do sit down, Emily. Have some wine.'

'Thank you.' She sank into one of the plush armchairs, and took a sip of the cool Sauterne Annabel poured for her, and didn't ask if it was Gerald's wine. Instead she made polite conversation. 'I have tried to have a word with Dashwood about the property on your behalf. He seems adamant at the moment, but I won't give up so soon.' Even as she spoke, Emily was positive that Andrew would not budge an inch to help the health clubs.

'Gerald is going to ask one of his Thai business friends for a loan—offer Dashwood more money, and maybe put some pressure on him.'

'Really?' It sounded nasty, but Emily kept quiet. This mix of politics and big business was out of her ken.

Annabel had recovered her poise. 'By the way, Gerald asked me to take you to my couturier. He said you need some clothes.'

'Oh, so he has mentioned my name?' Emily watched

Annabel's face, and wondered if behind the make-up she detected a flash of jealousy.

'Quite often, I assure you. Have you been very busy at the hospital?'

'Yes. Full-time for the past week, but things will get better now that they have isolated the source of infection. Several nurses have been told to stay away because they were contacts of a serious bacterium. Once they're back, I'll go part-time — and hopefully see more of Gerald. When is he due back?'

Annabel had looked bored at the hospital talk, but she looked more animated when Gerald's name was mentioned. Emily couldn't help feeling that Annabel was in love with him. The question was, what did Gerald feel about her? 'I expect him at Changi tomorrow night. Why don't we do dinner? The Shangri La would be nice — we haven't been there for ages. You'll like it, Emily. And why don't we go shopping tomorrow and buy you a decent gown.'

'I don't finish till six.'

'Then why not give me your measurements, and let me get you some designs on approval? Come round as soon as you finish, and you can get ready here.'

'You make it sound irresistible.'

'Good, then that's settled.'

Emily looked at the other woman dispassionately. 'You look after Gerald very well, Annabel. You're fond of him, aren't you? So why don't you try to get rid of me?'

For a moment Annabel looked vulnerable, but she soon covered it with her usual show of sophistication. 'If I tried to freeze you out, my dear, he'd hate me for it. At least this way I keep his friendship.'

'But I'm a thorn in your side?'

'Well, yes, a bit.' Annabel laughed suddenly, a high,

brittle laugh. 'But it's nothing personal, Emily. It was just a surprise when he came back from London and told us he'd met the ideal woman. I couldn't wait to meet you and find out what his idea of perfection was.'

'And I can tell you're not impressed.'

'Not true. You have a pretty face and lovely hair, and a nice figure. But Emily, forgive me if I say you are very innocent for your age.'

Emily smiled at her frankness. 'I don't know Singapore or the business world, Annabel, but I'm a fast learner.'

'That's what I'm afraid of.'

Emily sipped her wine, and said thoughtfully, 'I did love Gerald very much. He swept me off my feet. I couldn't wait to come out here to see him again. But there is a difference, and I think it will take a while to get to know him again. Especially if he isn't here so much. It won't be easy—but we owe it to ourselves to try again, not to give up at this stage. You do understand, don't you, Annabel?'

'I think so.'

'And you don't think it better for Gerald and me to see each other alone from time to time?'

'I suppose so.'

'Well, that's really what I came to say.'

Annabel poured more wine, and drank without speaking for a few moments. There was disappointment as well as thoughtfulness in her face. 'You're not as innocent as I thought.'

'No. I did tell you. But I want to be honest with you, and I hope you'll be the same with me.'

'I'll do my best.'

'So what are the arrangements for tomorrow?'

Realising Emily had won a small but significant victory, Annabel replied, 'I'll tell Gerald that you're calling straight from work, and you are going out together—just the two of you.'

'And we'll forget the dress for the moment?'

'Yes, Emily—come in whatever little thing you brought from London. I'm sure Gerald will like it.'

'If he doesn't, maybe you'll take me shopping next week?'

'Love to.'

Emily stood up. 'Well, make yourself at home.' She smiled. 'I'll see myself out.'

Annabel watched with cold eyes, and didn't get up from the sofa. Emily pressed the bell for the lift, and went out without looking back.

'They've isolated the troublesome Klebsiella bacterium, but we are still trying to find the source. Is there a carrier among the staff, or was it a patient who introduced the infection to the hospital?' Andrew Dashwood, in immaculate white coat, his mask pulled down under his chin, was briefing the ward staff in Sister Brown's office. 'And I'm glad to say that Marilyn Boon is out of danger. I'm sending her home in a couple of days to recuperate.'

Emily sighed with relief. 'Thank goodness. Poor Marilyn. But why did she have such a severe reaction? I thought Klebsiella was only dangerous to new babies and post-op patients—those with least natural resistance.'

Andrew said ruefully, 'There are over eighty serotypes. This one was the K pneumonia strain—causes Friedlander's pneumonia. Nasty, but very rare, thank goodness. But once it takes a hold it can spread in a warm hospital environment. So from now on we must all be extra careful to avoid any sources of infection, and, of course, to start antibiotic therapy early if there's any risk at all.'

'The infection is passed on by physical contact, isn't it?'

'Yes, usually. There's to be even more thorough hand-washing before and after dealing with patients. I understand the carrier may have been a porter who ought not to have been allowed into Intensive Care at all. I've rocketed them well and truly over the incident, and made sure the regulations are tightened up all round—thank goodness nobody vulnerable came to any harm.'

'Are we going to resume operating?' Emily asked. 'I'll have to start getting the patients in for pre-op tests.'

'Dr Mehtani and I have discussed it. We think it will be safe to start next Monday, with extra antibiotic cover.'

'Good. I'll start right away.'

Sue Brown said, 'No, Nurse Fairlie—leave the paperwork to a clerk. I want you back on the ward.'

'That's fine by me.'

'I'm afraid I still need you to work full-time.' Was that a glint of malice in her eye? During the emergency they had swallowed their differences, but now Emily saw that Sue was getting her own back. She must definitely have seen Emily going out with Andrew that night, and decided to make her displeasure plain.

The two boys in the ward welcomed Emily with whoops of delight. Kim was still waiting for his operation, while the older boy, Lennie, was ready to go home. His mother was with him, and she expressed her gratitude to Emily. 'He is a brave boy. He was born with water on the brain, and he has undergone many operations. But thanks to modern surgery he lives a normal life.'

'He has a lot of courage. And he has been a great friend to Kim.'

Lennie interrupted. 'I think I will be a surgeon when I grow up. I want to help boys like Kim. He was afraid of having an operation on his head, but now he sees me he knows there is nothing to fear. Surgeons are people who help.'

Emily said, 'Oh, Lennie, he will miss you when you go home.'

'But we will come back and see him after his operation—my mother has promised him.'

Kim said, importantly reciting what Lennie had taught him, 'It is not the same operation. Mine is to stop me having fits. Yours was to put a tube inside your head.'

Emily smiled in pity and admiration. She said to Lennie's mother, 'These two such small boys have learned the details of neurosurgery very young.'

'I agree, but being here has also taught them that it is nothing to be afraid of. Your staff are very kind, and the doctors very talented. It is a miracle to me that my son is so normal.'

Emily spoke optimistically to the mother. But she had also known the heartache of the little children who did not get better. She said nothing of this. Instead she said, 'I hope Lennie will go on and get his wish—to study surgery. This experience has given him a wisdom beyond his years. He will be a more understanding doctor because of it.'

Kim said, 'Your hair is beginning to grow, Lennie. Will mine grow fast afterwards?'

'Very fast. You will forget it was ever shaved off.' Encouraging words, and Kim smiled. But Emily saw him lift a hand and stroke his luxuriant glossy black hair. She made a mental note to be extra sympathetic about it after his operation, and to remind him often that he was still a handsome boy.

But this quiet little conversation was suddenly interrupted by loud noises in the corridor, and she could hear Sue Brown shouting, 'You're not allowed in this department. Please leave at once.'

The boys looked worried, so Emily led them to the window so that they could look out at the beautiful gardens. She said to the mother, 'Would you like to take the boys out to sit under the trees?' and the mother understood and chivvied them out into the sunshine.

Emily made her way back to the corridor. She was used to dealing with disruptive patients, and Sue sounded harassed. A tall Chinese with untidy hair and an aggressive look was standing outside Sue's office, and he was holding a video camera. He was saying in a rough voice, 'Our readers have a right to know if there is a dangerous outbreak of infection in a city hospital.'

A reporter. But how had he heard of the infection? Everyone had been sworn to secrecy, to prevent just exactly this type of scaremongering. Sue was saying, 'This is old news. There was one patient who was very ill, but she has recovered and gone home, and there haven't been any new cases. So go away, please. There's no story here.'

'I need to have that patient's name, ma'am. My editor will want me to check it out.'

Emily sized him up. He was a bully, and she knew how to deal with bullies. She came out of the ward wearing her mask, apron and rubber gloves, and pretended to be speaking privately to Sue. 'Has this young man been in the same room with "you-know-who"? And if so, how long has he got?'

Sue cottoned on to the subterfuge, and pulled up her mask. Her reply was low, but audible to the intruder.

'I'm afraid he's been breathing the same air. There isn't much hope.'

'What some people will do for a story. You have to admire them. I hope he hasn't got a family!'

'What — what are you saying? You're having me on!' But the reporter was looking distinctly green, and his voice shook. 'Who is this, Sister? She's British, isn't she? Have you called her in especially to deal with this problem?'

Emily turned to him. 'Who are you?'

The reporter muttered, 'It isn't — it isn't — AIDS?'

Both nurses burst out laughing. Emily went on, 'AIDS! If only it were — we could cope with that! Don't worry too much. I'm sure you're quite safe. But if the tips of your fingers start turning greenish, do let our medical team know at once.'

'You're — you're making fun of me.'

Sue shook her head in mock-seriousness. 'I wish we were, young man. I wish we were!'

Emily followed it up, like a fencer making a final plunge of the sword. 'I don't expect you — as a young man — would have thought what your final words were to be. Maybe now is a good time to start thinking about them — and maybe to start praying.'

'But — come off it, Sister! There are other people in this ward. . .'

'Other *protected* people. You barged in without checking whether it was safe to do so!'

Andrew Dashwood chose that very moment to walk by. 'Who is this?'

Emily pretended to be scared, and ran to pull Andrew's mask up over his nose and mouth. 'Oh, Doctor, this is a reporter. Do tell him that there's nothing to be afraid of! Only — he has been breathing without a mask!'

Andrew looked from the girls to the reporter and back again. He saw what they were planning, and played his part to perfection. 'I'm afraid you've been hoaxed. There's no story here, and I shall have words with these young ladies for frightening a stranger. Maybe it will serve to remind you very forcibly that hospitals can be dangerous places, and——' his voice was very grave, '—if you barge into a private ward in future the joke might just turn out to be serious.' He pulled his mask down, and quietly took the reporter's arm. The young man looked back, as Sue and Emily both took off their masks and laughed at him.

The reporter tried one last sally. 'But my information was kosher. There has been a story here.'

'There has been nothing here that doesn't happen in every hospital in the world at some time or another. No story, I'm afraid, and you've wasted your entire afternoon.'

Emily said innocently, 'And you'll spend the next year wondering just how much of a hoax it has been. Let it be a lesson to you.'

'The public have a right to know.'

'And our medical staff and our patients have a right to privacy. I hope you don't become a patient, but there is every chance that you might.'

Andrew said, 'Can I have your name? I think I ought to have a word with your editor——'

The young man and his camera melted away.

Andrew turned to Sue and smiled broadly. 'Well done. Bullies need to be taught a lesson. Now, is there anyone I need to see? Or can we share a pot of tea? I've been working all day, and missed lunch.'

Emily felt she wasn't wanted. It wouldn't be tactful to hang around these two. 'Excuse me, but I have something to do.'

Andrew laughed. 'You aren't staying to receive your Oscar? Pity. You both deserve one.'

Emily said, 'Would it be very serious if he reported a Klebsiella infection?'

'It wouldn't be a welcome thing. But thanks to you two he thinks he would be ridiculed if he reported it. Thanks again. I'm afraid—following widespread use of antibiotics—this situation could occur at any time in any hospital. So many bugs are resistant.'

Emily wanted to go on with the conversation, but the sight, from the corner of her eye, of Sue Brown hovering and waiting for Emily to disappear hastened her decision to return to the ward. 'I have temps and BPs to do.'

She took longer than usual doing the rounds, because all the patients wanted to discuss Marilyn's recovery, and to be reassured that there was no danger in recommencing operations. One apprehensive lady confided, 'They've done all my tests. There is a lump as big as a lemon inside my head. Can you believe it, Nurse? So big, and I have had no symptoms except an attack of double vision.'

'It isn't malignant, Mrs Tang. Once it's out, you should be fine.'

'But——'

'It's commoner than you think. I know—brain surgery seems such a frightening thing. But these days the surgeons in Singapore are very highly trained. Our surgical staff all have UK or US experience. Mr Mehtani is quite wonderful. We have some of the best in the world. You will look back on this experience the way people look back on having an appendix out, I promise you. It was nothing, you'll say.'

'But I have to take these pills?'

'Pre-op, yes. But only for a couple of weeks. You'll see—in a few days you will feel wonderful.'

'When I was a girl, brain surgery was a mystery.'

'Not any more.'

'My ancestors in Borneo used to believe that a camera could take away one's soul. What would they think of an operation inside the head?'

Emily smiled, and said gently, 'Your soul is safe, Mrs Tang. Only you have custody of that.'

Slowly Emily made her way back to the office. Her work was over, and soon she would be dressing for a date with her Gerald, the man she left home and job and family for. Thoughtfully, she recalled Annabel's admission of affection for Gerald. It was an obstacle, but Emily had a quiet confidence that if they were meant for each other she and Gerald would find out soon enough.

She was impatient to see him again. And she was a little hurt that he had not phoned her more. Annabel had explained that by saying Emily needed her space. More likely Annabel wanted the chance to insinuate herself into Gerald's affections, and had forced Gerald to leave her alone. Well, having seen for herself how Annabel lived, Emily had no intention of letting her have a clear run!

Her mind was going over what dresses she had in her wardrobe. She wanted to be stunning tonight, to have Gerald really appreciate her as a woman. And with a woman's intuition she knew that if she kept the dress simple he would be more likely to appreciate her bright hair and her slim figure. Lucky—she had a simple black that would do just that. Not a designer label by any means—but Emily was learning rapidly how to make the most of her best points.

She was brought out of her reverie by the sound of

raised voices in the office. Andrew was still there, and he was arguing with Sue, who was saying plaintively, 'You didn't need to take her for a drink!'

'I didn't need to take you out for dinner last Saturday either, but I did, and we both enjoyed it!' Andrew was trying to be logical.

'You're going to break my heart, Andrew.'

'My dear, that's not my intention. I want you to be happy — and you know I don't want to be tied down.'

'I know that well enough. You never stop telling me! But one day you must, and I believe I'm the one for the job.'

His lovely voice hardened. 'Allow me to make my own mind up about that. And Sue, poppet, don't spoil it all by being jealous.'

Emily had stopped, her back to the door, for too long already, but she dared not move in case Sue saw her outline passing the window. 'I'm not jealous of Emily Fairlie. God know she's already spoken for, and anyway, she's very thin. You like a woman with a figure. I know that, darling.'

There was a low chuckle from behind the frosted glass, and a rustle that sounded very much like an embrace. She thought she heard him say, 'Eight o'clock tonight?' Emily held her breath. They were a couple, that was for sure, in spite of Andrew's protestations of wanting his freedom. She would remember that in future.

She bumped into Andrew rather hard as he came out of the office in a rush. 'Oh, I'm so sorry,' they both said together.

'Emily, where have you been?'

'Doing the temps — and chatting to the patients. I'm off duty in a moment.'

Sue came to the door, fixing her cap. She wasn't

angry any more. 'Oh, Emily, thanks again for helping me get rid of that pest of a reporter.'

'No problem.'

'Going out tonight?'

Emily nodded, knowing it would be pure honey to Sue's ears. 'Yes, I'm meeting my fiancé.'

She saw Andrew's face darken. He hated Gerald, and didn't bother to hide it. She recalled their first meeting, when the name of Gerald Montague sent Andrew striding off in the opposite direction. But tonight he said nothing, and Emily was able to take her leave of them both politely, and start the scented walk across the lawns to the bungalow.

She had reached the hidden part, where someone had thoughtfully provided a rustic wooden bench. She caught her breath when she saw Andrew sitting there, a medical journal in his hands, his white coat swinging open, as though he had been there for hours. She was conscious of his thrusting masculine figure, the muscular legs crossed and his fitted shirt showing off his triangular chest going up from lean waist to smooth, broad shoulders. She caught her breath, his nearness and his perfection again grabbing her by the throat when she had thought herself immune. She approached him quietly, knowing that his sky-blue eyes would capture her as soon as he lifted his head from his magazine.

But he didn't lift his head. 'Emily!' He was still pretending to read. 'Where are you going with Gerald?'

'I've no idea. And it's no business of yours.'

'He's going to tell you what a worthless chap I am, hanging on to that plot of land — and you're going to believe him.'

She had to stop, directly in front of him. 'Oh, stop

pretending to read! And how did you get here before me? Face me, you coward!'

Slowly he closed the journal and looked up, and in spite of being prepared for it his blue gaze captivated her by its sheer handsomeness. She had thought of a string of cutting comments, and was ready to deliver them, but his physical presence was too much for her, and she opened her mouth, only to find herself saying, 'You shouldn't!'

He stood up, unfolding his length and standing very close to her, so that the warmth of his body matched the heat of the night. 'Shouldn't what?'

'Make use of your sex appeal.'

His hands were gripping her shoulders now, and his eyes searched her face. 'But it's the only way to get you to take some notice of me, Emily.'

'I—don't want to take any notice of you—except to persuade you to sell the—land. . .' But her voice had become weaker and fainter as his lips touched her forehead as lightly as a butterfly. At once they were kissing, and it was as though neither of them could help it. His mouth was soft but demanding, and he caught her lips and her tongue inside his lips, sweeter than honey and just as addictive. His arms tightened around her, and she felt her own arms embrace his body, loving the lean perfection of him, and the magic influence of his persistent kisses. 'Andrew——'

'Yes, little Emily?' His lips brushed her forehead as he spoke, and sent yet more tendrils to parts of her body not yet used to being invaded so blatantly.

She swallowed, and managed to whisper, 'This is wrong—not here—not now.'

'Shall I see you home?' he murmured into her hair.

'No.'

'But I can't resist any longer.'

'I think — you can — '

'Emily. . .' and his voice wafted into her consciousness with a liquid delight that turned her resolve to water. . . 'I've never met a girl like you. I'd be crazy to let you go. Let's go home?'

'Andrew — ' Suddenly she recalled his embrace with Sue, and his whispered assignation, and it gave her unexpected strength. 'Andrew, go away. If I'd wanted this, I would have told you.'

'Are you sure?' And his smile told her he knew she was lying.

She stiffened as she felt gentle pressure from his fingers, looked up at him until he slowly took his hands from her shoulders, let them fall to his sides. Emily said, trying to be firm, 'I know so little about you. I'm not sure I know anything at all about you — except that you are a good doctor, and that you belong to the board of SEAH even though you seem to go against all that they stand for.'

Andrew suddenly swung back to the seat, sat down, and patted the space next to him. 'I'll explain if you'll let me.'

Her curiosity got the better of her judgement, and she sat down at his side, though making sure they were not touching. 'I'd like that.'

'I'm on the board because they needed a medical adviser. I'm well-known for looking after some of the top people in Singapore — word of mouth mostly, because I never advertise. I think Gerald thought I would be a yes-man because we're the same nationality. I'm afraid the Haw Sing project showed him where my priorities lie. I'm a Singaporean, Emily. All right, my folks were from England. They worked here — for an oil company. They sent me to school and university in London. But after housemanship and gaining my

MRCP I came back — via jobs in Thailand and Australia for a little variety. I belong here now. My roots and my inclination are the same — Singaporean.'

'Your parents ——'

'I was a late child. They're both dead.'

'Are you rich, Andrew? All the doctors I've seen here are wealthy men.'

Andrew smiled. 'No doubt the Hon. Gerald has told you I live in a dump! Well, that's from choice. Yes, I earn a very reasonable income indeed and, as I've been working for over ten years, naturally I should have a comfortable sufficiency. But I spent my parents' legacy on property, and I now spend my income on the upkeep of that property. I need very little, Emily, to be happy. Just my work, and some good friends around me. . .'

He was looking quizzically at her, and Emily shook her head. 'You're a mystery still.'

'There's no mystery about the way I feel about you!'

She bypassed his remark. 'When you say you bought property, I expect you mean the Haw Sing building?'

'That's right.'

'But you could sell it for much more than you paid for it.'

'I could. But I won't.'

'You own the entire place?'

'Yes. And I need every rental from every shop and office in that building to keep it going.'

'Andrew, why keep it?'

'Maybe one day I'll tell you.'

'Not now?'

He stood up and stood in front of her. She was awed suddenly by the earnestness in his face. Although his features were youthful, she saw now the lines of anxiety at the corners of his clear blue eyes, the touch of silver in the rich, shining hair over his temples, and realised he must be older than he looked. He reached out one hand and very gently caressed her cheek with a feather touch. He said, with a slight shake of his head, 'Oh, Emily, you're so wasted on Montague. When will you realise that?' She whispered that he was only a playboy, and he blew her a kiss, turned on his heel, striding away without looking back.

To Sue Brown. Emily had heard that assignation all too clearly. Eight o'clock tonight... Emily walked slowly back to her flat, glad that she had not given way to his murmured suggestions, but still curious how he could sound so passionate while already dating someone else. Oh, yes, Andrew Dashwood was a man to avoid. He was too charming for his own good, and she was already too vulnerable in her affair with Gerald. Another man in her life would be just too much.

CHAPTER SIX

THE telephone was ringing in her flat, and Emily's key rattled in the lock as she struggled to calm herself and let herself in. It was Gerald, and his voice was deep and steady and somehow comforting. 'You came to see me, darling! That was a nice surprise.'

'Yes!' She squeaked the word, and tried again, her emotions still playing tricks with her, and her body still warm and tingling after Andrew Dashwood's forceful and impulsive embraces. He was a strong man and a passionate one, a combination not easy to forget. 'Yes, Gerald. I hope you don't mind. We—haven't seen much of each other.'

'I'm very happy, Emily. I'll send Chang for you, shall I? Half an hour?'

Half an hour. Was that enough to shake off all lingering traces of Andrew's closeness? 'All right. I'll just have a shower and slip into something—less medical.' His reaction was positive, and she ventured to add, 'I hope you got on well in Bangkok?'

'Quite satisfactory, darling. I'll tell you all about it. By the way, Annabel is refusing to join us. Don't you think that's tactful of her?'

'Jolly tactful.' Emily found herself speaking in the same plummy voice used by Annabel and Gerald, and she smiled at herself. She didn't really fit into their world yet—but perhaps it was all a matter of time before she was assimilated.

After the shower, she noticed with alarm that there was a small red mark on her neck. Her cheeks flushed.

It was where Andrew had kissed her just a little bit too enthusiastically. She touched it, her cheeks grew warm and her eyes misted as she recalled her abandoned response to his sweet lips. If she had allowed it, he would have followed her inside. Only the evocation of Sue Brown's wrath had made him reluctantly turn away, and swear that next time he would choose a more suitable place of assignation. 'You're nothing but a playboy, Andrew Dashwood!' she had hissed at him, and he had laughed, blown her a kiss, and walked away into the night. She touched the kiss on her neck, and tried not to admit to herself that a part of her longed for him to be there and to repeat his audacious behaviour.

But it was as Gerald's fiancée that she dressed in a fitted black dress, put small diamonds in her ears, and fluffed out her abundant fair hair over her shoulders, where it fortunately hid the mark of Andrew's kiss. She looked at her left hand, bare of rings, and wondered if one day she would wear Gerald's diamond. But no, not if she allowed Andrew Dashwood to have such an effect on her again. She wasn't ready for an engagement, if another man could play such havoc with her desires and emotions. Annoyed with herself now, she sat up straight, and determined to play her part to the letter. Gerald was the reason she had come to Singapore. Gerald was the man she would spend the evening with, and she would allow her wayward thoughts no more leeway.

He was waiting in the apartment, debonair in his dinner-jacket, his waving dark hair slicked back, and a look of real interest in his aristocratic brown eyes. He held out both hands, and went to her. 'Darling, you are a sight for sore eyes.'

'You too, Gerald.' His embrace was warm, and his

kiss more so, bringing back memories of their first romantic evenings in London. 'It's nice to have you to myself for once.'

'I thought you needed your space?'

'Just in my job, Gerald. I only want room to be myself.'

'How is the nursing profession, darling?' He had apparently forgotten his opposition to her work.

'We've been through a sticky time — there's been a bad infection in the ward, but it's all over now.' She noticed that Gerald's grip on her waist eased suddenly at the mention of infection, and she hastened to reassure him that it was nothing that couldn't be controlled. 'It's all over now,' she repeated. 'And I wasn't involved. But we had to work very hard. I'm so glad we can relax tonight.'

He smiled again, and poured champagne, and they sat on the cream satin sofa together while Gerald decided where to eat. 'Annabel thought we would like the Shangri La. She's booked us a table, but if you like we could go to the Raffles.'

'No, thanks. I was there last week.'

'Who with?' Again that sharp look of distrust, that hint of uncertainty.

'Dashwood. I was trying to persuade him to sell.'

'Oh.' Again Gerald's hand loosened on hers, and she realised that he was very insecure about her, unsure whether she really cared for him — and quite possibly not sure if he wanted her back. It was going to be a long haul, learning to like and to trust each other again.

She said, 'Tell me about Bangkok. Annabel said you had someone there who could help to persuade Dashwood to sell. More money, was it?'

'More than that.' Gerald looked pleased with himself. 'Come on, let's go and eat. I feel like oysters and steak. How about you?'

'I'm a novice here. I'll wait to see the menu.'

'There's absolutely no need, darling. They'll get you whatever you fancy. They value my custom.'

Emily laughed. 'I'll need some time to get used to a culture like that. Maybe I'll just have what you have.'

'Fine. Let's go, then.'

In the elegant restaurant she felt very strongly that Gerald was showing her off, treating her like an accessory. She was aware that she didn't let him down, the black dress showing her pretty legs to advantage, and her hair a positive plus under the crystal chandeliers. But although there was self-satisfaction there was no personal warmth in Gerald's eyes. He chatted at her, not to her, and he occasionally looked around, to see if anyone who mattered was there that night.

'About Bangkok——' He leaned over and spoke quietly. 'There is a member of the government—an old Etonian like myself—who knew Dashwood as a young man.'

'He's not exactly old.'

'You know what I mean—knew him while he was a student and as junior doctor—a bit of a wild man, so I'm told.' Gerald winked. 'Got up to some tricks with older women. A bit flash, as a student. Given his looks, I suppose it's easy to do—and doesn't it give me the upper hand when asking a favour from him!'

Emily stared. 'Surely you don't mean—you aren't going to *blackmail* him, are you?'

'Don't be ridiculous, darling. What a word to use! No, but a word from someone who did know him in his student days might remind him of the debt he owes to society.'

'Society, yes—but why to the South East Asia Health

Clubs?' This whole thing was beginning to sound sordid. Was this really the way grown men did business?

Gerald leered over his glass, and she wondered why she had ever thought him handsome. 'A little knowledge is a useful thing!'

Emily felt cheated. She didn't think she liked Andrew Dashwood very much — although she acknowledged his strong physical appeal, and could not deny the volcano he aroused in her when he desired. But she did admire him as a good doctor, and felt unhappy at the thought that Gerald would stoop to blackmail to get his own way. She said, 'Just leave me out of it, then.'

Gerald looked at her sharply. 'You're either with us or against us, my love. I can't have you in on our secrets unless we know you are one hundred per cent loyal.'

'I won't tell tales, if that's what you mean.'

'I might expect more from you than that.'

'No, Gerald.'

Emily sat on her bed that night, too tired and disappointed to take off the black dress and the diamond earrings. She had had such high hopes of tonight — it was going to be the start of a new relationship with Gerald. But he had shattered her dream almost before the evening had started. Blackmail. . . It was a nasty word, and one she would never have expected to hear from the man she had once hoped to marry.

The phone rang suddenly, startling her, and she picked it up, expecting it to be a wrong number. 'Emily, thank goodness you're back.'

It was Andrew Dashwood, and he sounded upset. Emily bit back the annoyance that Gerald had awoken in her and said, 'Is something wrong?'

'It's little Kim — he's in status epilepticus. Fit after fit since four this afternoon. I thought you should know, Emily. I've done what I can, but if you don't mind —'

'Of course I'll come. And Andrew —'

'Yes?'

'Send for Lennie's mother.'

Andrew didn't ask why. Emily tore off the cocktail dress and pulled her uniform over her head as she made for the door. When the boy came round, he would expect a familiar figure, not a dressed-up society lady. She ran across the path to the hospital, and found Dr Dashwood standing over the unconscious little figure of Kim. He said, 'The fits have eased, thank God. We should have operated last week. Damn that Klebsiella. Mehtani should have gone ahead with the operation, and we could have arranged for him to be nursed in a different ward.'

Emily stood beside him, catching her breath, and they both gazed down at the child. He was lying on his side, breathing very deeply, and there was a drip in his arm. It was easy to say what should have been done — after the event. The other bed was empty, as Lennie had already gone home. She said, 'There must be something organic to account for this?'

'Something that didn't show up at investigation, then. Either that, or he hasn't taken his medication.'

'I always made sure he took his pills. It was easy when Lennie was with him, because the one encouraged the other.'

'Is that why you asked me to send for Lennie's mother?'

'Yes. Kim's parents are in China, and he lives with a rather austere grandmother. He has an aunt but she's on holiday on a remote island in Malaysia and can't be contacted. Lennie's mother had taken a fancy to Kim — I believe he'll need her when he comes round.'

'If——' But there was no need for Andrew to spell it out.

'He's had a CT scan and EEG, I know. How about lumbar puncture?'

'I thought I'd leave the cerebrospinal fluid until later, poor little chap. I don't believe there's a neoplasm, though Mehtani's diagnosis was fits due to scars following birth trauma. His father is epileptic—well-controlled on Tegretol. No, I think there's been some mix-up in his tablets. Anyway, I've asked Mehtani to consider an operation the day after tomorrow, as soon as he's recovered from this. I've given him paraldehyde, and intramuscular sodium phenobarb when the fits eased, and it seems to have done the trick.'

'Poor little fellow. Well, I'll sit with him if you like. Are you putting up a monitor?'

'Yes—any change at all and I'm to be called.'

'That's OK.'

'And Emily——'

'Yes?'

'Thank you for coming. I know you're off duty. Lucky you were in when I called.' A monitor was wheeled in, and Kim's limp little body was connected to the machine. Andrew switched it on, and the even lines of heart-rate and blood-pressure began to bleep out into the silent ward.

Emily took her place at the side of the bed, where she could see both the monitor and the patient's face. 'I was only just in.'

'Gerald?'

'Yes, as a matter of fact.'

Andrew grinned to himself, and tried to hide it. She said, irritated, 'What does the sly smile mean? I haven't said anything amusing, as far as I know.'

'Just that I'm very glad Gerald didn't keep you out late.'

'That isn't your business.'

'No — except that if you and Gerald had — gone back to his place — you wouldn't be here to help me, and I'd have had to call Sue.'

'Would that make a difference?'

'It would to Sue,' he replied enigmatically, and he scribbled his treatment on Kim's notes before strolling out of the ward. 'Bleep me immediately if there's any change,' were his final words.

Mrs Wang came in later, her kindly face anxious. 'How is the little boy?'

'Better.'

'They said he had a bad fit.'

'He had several fits in a row, Mrs Wang, and it could have been fatal. He needs urgent surgery, and I thought perhaps you wouldn't mind — his grandmother is very old and frail ——'

'Of course I don't mind. You wanted someone he knew to be here when he wakes?'

'Yes. He will be bewildered at first, and I thought two familiar faces would be reassuring. Do sit down. I'll organise some tea for you.' She went into the office, where one of the night staff had already made tea and poured two mugs for Emily to take.

It was a long night, and the little boy's breathing remained deep and harsh at times. But slowly, as dawn began to brighten the little ward with slits of rose-pink through the Venetian blind, Kim stirred and moaned a little. Emily looked at the monitor. No change, but perhaps Andrew ought to be informed. She called the night nurse. 'Let Dr Dashwood know that Kim is regaining consciousness, and his EEG is steady.'

'Yes, Staff Nurse.'

The child opened his eyes, and a smile lit up his face.
'Mrs Wang, why are you here?'

'I came to see if you were all right.'

'Is Lennie with you?'

'No, he's asleep at home. His father is with him.'

'Will Lennie come?'

'Of course.' The motherly soul reached out and took Kim's hand. 'Just tell me what you need, my dear, and Aunty Wang will get it for you.'

Later, when Emily had given Mrs Wang her warmest thanks and seen her to the door, Andrew came back, and he declared Kim to be over the worst. The child had fallen back to sleep, but it was now a natural rest, and his colour had returned to normal. Andrew said, 'OK, Emily — thanks for standing in. And for that brainwave of fetching Mrs Wang. I believe it made all the difference. Go and grab some rest now, and don't come back on duty until the afternoon.'

'Thanks.' She was extremely tired now, her eyes sore and trying to close, but somehow it was easier to care for a sick child than it was to be left alone with her thoughts. Gerald and his unpleasant ideas drifted back into her mind. Could he really mean to blackmail Andrew into submission? And Annabel — sweetly spoken, bottle-blonde Annabel, with her artificial niceness and her narrowed, calculating eyes. Work with her little people like Kim was a lot more rewarding than mixing with people like that. And yet — she wasn't going to give up on Gerald yet. He might be all talk. She would have to wait and see.

She had reached her own door when Andrew caught up with her, and he caught her off guard, so that while she was wishing him a goodnight he was already inside the door and closing it behind them. Outside, the garden was misty with morning dew, the sky translucent like stretched silk in front of a candle. The crickets had ceased their night chorus, the palm trees were silhouetted against the sky, and there was a heavenly stillness hanging over the garden, breathless with hope, as there must have been on the morning that the Garden of Eden was created.

She was too weary to argue with Andrew now. 'You think we've won?'

'I think so. It's up to Mehtani now.' He sank down into a chair and leaned his head back. He wasn't wearing a white coat, just a crumpled polo shirt and trousers, and his hair was tousled. She noticed that again he had that shimmer of stubble on his chin, that stubble that had grazed against her so enticingly, the last time they had met in the garden.

Emily said, 'Why don't you go home?'

'This one has a better-looking tenant.' His voice was still tired, but there was a hint of a growl in it that threatened her peace of mind. 'Sit by me, Emily? Stroke my brow?'

'You have a cheek. You make me work all night, and then you march into my house uninvited and expect sexual favours on top of all that. Go home, Andrew, and come back when you're less of a chauvinist.'

He rolled his head to one side and opened one eye. 'Don't you want me to stroke your brow?'

'Certainly not. I want you to take your behind off my chair and leave me to sleep.'

With a sudden unwinding, like a springing panther, he sat up and put his elbows on his knees and leaned forward, his lovely eyes wide and searching. 'Emily, what did Gerald say about me? Did you quarrel about me? Is that why you came home alone? Early?'

Emily was shaken awake by the suddenness of the question. 'Look, I don't want to talk about SEAH any more today. You won't sell your precious plot, so that's that. I just — well, if you want my opinion it seems crazy not to let them have it.'

'Did he ask you to say that?'

Emily tried to prevaricate. 'He obviously hopes I'll be on his side.'

'But——?' Oh, why did his face look so perfect, one sculpted eyebrow quizzically raised, and that gentle smile touching his warm, inviting lips?

She did her best to ignore his beauty, his subtle animal magnetism. 'But I'm tired, and you are like a terrier — I know you won't give up, so I'd be wasting my time if I prolonged this conversation.'

'But I need to know, Emily. Why didn't you go back to his place for soft lights and champagne?'

'That has nothing at all to do with you.'

'I think it has.'

'Andrew, get out before I commit justifiable homicide with the bread knife!'

Andrew stood up and drew her, unwittingly at first, into his arms. His face was very close, his voice was very soft and his eyes were very bright as they gazed into hers. 'What did he say that has made you so defensive, Emily?'

The word 'blackmail' hovered in the air. She could almost read the letters. But some residual loyalty was due to Gerald, and she said nothing. Nothing must be said until she was sure Gerald was going to carry out his threat. That didn't stop Andrew kissing her.

She fought him with what strength she had left, snatching her head away so that her hair swung over her face and shoulders, wild and free. 'Why did you do that?'

'Because the day is beautiful and so are you. And because at this time of day I've no resistance to beauty.'

The sparrows sang in the eaves, and the hummingbirds in the hibiscus. Emily was by now so weary and languid that she had little resistance herself to the magic he knew how to work with his lips. And why fight him, when they had worked together so well tonight and felt the satisfaction that only came when you saw a child recover? Andrew Dashwood was a complex character, but he intrigued her and at times he excited her by his looks and easy, teasing manner. If only she could have met him somewhere else.

But she was here in Singapore because of Gerald Montague, and there were shreds of their past affair that reminded her that Gerald didn't deserve to be treated dishonourably. . . But then, under the persistent nuzzling of Andrew's mouth and tongue, his murmured pleas and hoarse, fragmented compliments, Emily was gradually made to forget Gerald Montague totally, and she wound her arms round Andrew's neck and kissed him as she had longed to do since he had first aroused her secret, throbbing senses.

'Hey, kid, do that again,' Andrew moaned breathlessly, his mouth against her ear. 'Do it again, please?'

'No.' She ought not to have allowed herself that momentary lapse. But Andrew did it for her, capturing her mouth in his and coaxing a response from her, so that for a long time they stood, swaying, embracing, enchanted. Every inch of her inner body had sprung into life, and the longer they stood, the more she felt conscious of the outlines of his very masculine, very aroused anatomy, and the more aware of her own urgent need to do something about it.

'Emily, there's never been anyone like you in my life.' The words were whispered, and she didn't hear them all because of the pulsing of blood in her ears. But she knew there was a reason why this couldn't go on, and as she tried to remember it she brought both her hands in front of his chest, feeling the outline of his muscles — and tried to push him away.

His reply was to bring both his hands and place them squarely over her breasts. His touch made her gasp, but she tried to disguise her reaction by tossing back her hair with one hand. His fingers were gentle but probing over the softness of her, and she felt herself needing him more. He smiled at her dishevelled face. 'Want me to push you away?'

'Andrew, this isn't happening. We've both — been too long without sleep.'

'So, let's sleep. You have a bed?' He stroked her breasts, and then gently caressed her body before putting his arms back around her waist.

'I do indeed have a bed, Andrew, but I don't enjoy being conned into it.'

'Darling, who's doing the conning?'

For the first time she paused to think. Yes, she had made him think she wanted him. 'I probably deserved that. Andrew, whatever it is you want, you won't get it here. Is that clear enough? I apologise for misleading you, but I think it was more your fault — and the fact that I'm asleep on my feet.'

The piercing sound of his bleep interrupted the sweet banter of their conversation. With a groan, Andrew picked up her telephone to check with the ward. Then he turned to her. 'There's a problem in ENT. God help us if it's Klebsiella again.'

'Oh, Andrew, no!'

'Sounds like it.' He smoothed his hair back with a vulnerable air. 'Someone from Intensive Care. That's where the resistant bugs are coming from, I'm afraid.' He took a step towards the door, and then turned back, to see Emily rubbing her eyes and forehead with trembling fingers. His sharp concern was plain, but she pretended she didn't see it, with a modest downward look. 'Em—you think that Andrew Dashwood is no gentleman, don't you?'

'I think I've worked that out for myself, Andrew.' But her voice was soft. How could she blame Andrew for her own weakness? She took a deep breath and stood upright. Back in control of her own emotions, she could be magnanimous. 'I don't want you to come to my flat again. I mean it. But as a colleague you can call me as and when you need me. I hope you remember that.'

He gave a little smile, and ran his fingers over his whiskers. 'Where would we be without our— colleagues?'

'Get lost, Dashwood!'

But she watched him walking into the bushes before she closed the door. At least she could sleep now, while Andrew was called back to duty. It wasn't an easy life, and she felt for him. She closed the door slowly, and wondered who the 'older woman' was who had figured in his student life.

She went into work in the afternoon. Sue was offhand with her, carefully refusing to praise her or thank her for staying with Kim all night. Emily began to suspect why. Andrew had come straight to her flat, not bothering to check if anyone saw him. The news must have got to Sue. Later, as they stood together over a new patient, Sue was saying, 'This gentleman has been admitted for investigations, Nurse Fairlie, but the initial diagnosis is Parkinsonism—as you could probably see.'

'Yes, he has a coarse tremor of both hands.'

'He is due for further investigation. If you could keep your claws off Dr Dashwood for a few moments, I'll give him a buzz and ask him to examine and advise what tests to organise.'

'That wasn't very nice.'

'Your behaviour isn't very nice, Nurse Fairlie. I thought you were an engaged woman. Your fiancé won't know of your antics with our consultant, I'm sure.'

Emily took a deep breath and tried to be calm. 'I didn't ask Dr Dashwood to my flat, and he only stayed a few moments. We — discussed the case, if you must know.'

'I bet!' Sue tossed her head in a most unsisterly way, and went to telephone Andrew. Emily did her best to forget the atmosphere between them, by bending down and chatting to the worried patient, a middle-aged Indian who said he was a retired teacher.

Andrew came to examine him, and she saw him pause when he discovered her in the room. For a long moment their eyes met, and neither of them moved. Then Sue Brown came in with a sheaf of notes, and Emily turned to leave. But Andrew's eyes followed her, and she felt the heat of his body as she passed him. It was then that she knew she had fallen in love with him.

CHAPTER SEVEN

IT WAS embarrassing to realise that she was shatteringly, deeply in love with Gerald's antagonist. It was embarrassing, inconvenient, and awkward. But Emily couldn't help it. From the first moment she had set eyes on Andrew Dashwood he had fascinated her. Now that she had worked with him, cared for patients and discussed their welfare with him, she knew his mind, skill, his compassion and his intellect were wholly admirable. But she didn't know anything about his background, except those few brief words the other night. In a way that was good, because there must be some bad about him, and that would certainly shake her out of this ridiculous fantasy. Perplexed, Emily sat in the nurses' rest-room and sipped coffee that had gone cold as she pondered. She had come to Singapore to fall in love. But it was the wrong man.

Sue Brown was not in uniform. She wore a sleek figure-hugging dress in green shot moiré. Her rather sparse fair hair was brushed neatly, falling into a bob over lightly made-up cheeks. She walked over to Emily and stood squarely in front of her table. 'We have to talk.'

'Yes, Sister.'

'No, not using rank. As women, we have to talk.'

Emily's heart sank. She had just realised she was desperately in love, and now she had to face Andrew's official girlfriend. How cruel could life be? She said, 'Sit down, then, Sue. I'm not sure what I can say that can help.'

Sue sat rigidly on the edge of a chair, and Emily felt sorry for the look of hopelessness on her face. Sue said, 'You probably know by now that Andrew and I have been together for quite a while.'

Emily said at once, 'I don't want Andrew Dashwood. I swear to you I don't.'

'That's rich. A guy like Andrew doesn't come along very often, and you say you don't want him!'

'What I mean is, I don't want to come between you and him. I mean it, Sue. I came to Singapore because of Gerald — Gerald Montague, the health club man. We met in London last year. We're almost engaged.'

'So how come Andrew spends his entire time off in your flat?'

'That's an exaggeration.'

'Is it? Then how come he used to spend all his spare time in my flat, and since you came he hasn't been once?'

Emily tried to cool things, though she knew Sue was right. 'We've had the Klebsiella thing. He's been working all the hours God sends.'

'And cooling off — or is it warming up? — in your place!'

Emily knew it was true. But how to tell Sue? She did her best to be diplomatic, to think before she spoke. 'Don't you think that Andrew is a bit of a free spirit? Maybe he comes to me because I don't want to tie him down? I made it clear to him that Gerald matters to me.'

'I'd say it was more likely to excite him. He likes a challenge.'

'Rubbish, Sue. I'm sorry, but I think you're crowding him. If you ease up, I think he'll like you better.'

'I don't mind easing up if I knew you weren't going to go behind my back.'

'I swear it.'

'You swear you haven't slept with him?'

Emily exploded. 'Sue! I hardly know the man.'

'And will you sleep with him when you know him?'

Emily didn't reply at once, but she saw the titanic emotions that were tearing Sue apart. 'I wish you would believe me when I tell you I know how you feel. But you're going after the wrong person. I never invited Andrew to my place, and he's only been once. Nothing happened, Sue.'

The other woman looked down, suddenly looking vulnerable and lost. 'Andrew likes a challenge, Emily. If you hold out on him, he'll never leave you alone. But when he gets what he wants, you'll be down on the list of has-beens.'

Emily sighed. 'Your Dr Dashwood is only another doctor to me — someone who makes the diagnosis, prescribes the drugs, that sort of thing. I work with him, otherwise I wouldn't see him. And——' she crossed her fingers then, secretly '— Sue, I don't want to see him. OK?'

Sue shrugged, still looking dejected. 'I won't tell him that. It'll only make him keener.'

'Then get off his back, Sue. Give him his elbow-room. He'll like you the better for it.'

The other girl stood up. Her eyes narrowed in scorn. 'You'd like that, wouldn't you? Give him space so that he can come to your room whenever he wants! Oh, no, Emily Fairlie, you're not getting him as easily as that! I care for that man, and I won't let go just because you tell me to. I can make him happy, I know I can.'

Irritated, Emily said, 'Then I wish you luck.'

'That's cruel.'

'Is it?'

'Yes — you've got him and I haven't.'

'I haven't got him, and I promise I won't encourage him. Will that suit you?'

'Smug pommie. You haven't heard the last of this, you know.'

'Sue——'

But Sue Brown was already striding away. Distressed at the scene, Emily stared after her—only to watch her emerge into the sunlight and almost collide with Andrew Dashwood, white coat-tails flying, as he crossed the lawn on the way to the clinic. He grinned, and held out a hand to steady her. Emily watched as Sue looked up. Andrew saw her face, and she was crying. He put his hand on her shoulder, in natural sympathy, only to find Sue throwing herself into his arms.

Emily knew she ought not to be watching, but she couldn't take her eyes away. She saw Andrew patting Sue's shoulders, and slowly coaxing her to look up. Then, gently, he led her away, his arm still loosely on her shoulder, and his other hand stroking her hair from her eyes. It was a tender scene, and it gave Emily a real insight into Sue's violent emotions. There was a genuine long-standing relationship here, and, whether Andrew knew it or not, it was plain that he did care for Sue quite a lot.

She began to despise him a little—he had no right to come to her flat when another woman believed him to be hers. Emily began to think over what Gerald had told her—Andrew Dashwood could so easily have had many such females in the past. He seemed to have that effect on women, and over the years could have upset many of them. When he was a student, it was quite conceivable that he had bewitched someone important to fall for him. Blackmail might be a dirty word, but it was possible that there were grounds for it.

Next morning on the noticeboard Emily saw that she had been put on full-time for the next three weeks. So that was Sue's revenge. But at least she had three days off now. She must make sure she spent as much time as possible with Gerald. If only she could be sure that he was alone. But Annabel seemed to be always at his elbow, and a love-affair couldn't be rekindled in such circumstances.

She went to his office at the Tanglin Palace hotel. A Chinese secretary told her he was at the health club next door, and Emily decided to take this golden opportunity to catch him without Annabel. 'You are a member, madam?' the slender sylph at the desk asked.

Emily replied, undaunted, 'Not yet, but I hope to be.'

'Can I take your name, madam?'

'Yes. I'm Emily Fairlie — a close friend of Mr Gerald Montague. I understand he's here?'

The pretty face went blank. 'I'm not sure.'

Emily saw through her — Gerald had given orders not to be disturbed unless he wanted it. 'Maybe you'd find him for me?'

'It isn't——'

Emily interrupted, putting on her best accent, 'He would be most annoyed if he knew I'd been here and he missed me.'

'I'll have him paged, madam.' And within seconds the chauffeur Chang appeared, and asked Emily to go with him.

Gerald was in the hot jacuzzi. His hair was damp, and he was wearing very brief trunks. She had been right — he was getting a tummy, and obviously was now trying to do something about it. 'Emily! What are you doing here?'

'Looking for you.'

'That's marvellous. I say, darling, you wouldn't be free tonight, would you?'

'Yes, as a matter of fact.'

Gerald leapt from the pool, dripping. He took her face in his hot, wet hands, and kissed her with considerable enthusiasm. 'Jolly good, jolly good. Look, sweetie, we'll go to my room and I'll tell you why it's so splendid.'

'You're having friends round?'

He beamed. 'One doesn't talk about friends in business circles, sweet. There are just colleagues you trust and colleagues you don't.'

'And tonight?'

'The SEAH, sweetie — the full board. I'm delighted they're going to have the pleasure of meeting you. Think you can cope, darling?'

'I can't wait.'

'Ah — but what about a decent gown? Think Annie ought to take you to her dressmaker?'

'No.'

'Sweetheart, why?'

'Gerald, I'm very glad you have a reliable PA, but ever since I arrived in Singapore Annabel has been wrapping you in cotton wool. When are we going to be alone?'

'We were last night, sweetie. It was you who said you were tired and sent me home.'

'You know that was because I didn't like the way you talked about blackmail.'

'Ah — well, Dashwood will be coming tonight.'

'The board meeting?'

'Yes, he's as much right to be there as the rest of us — even though he's being a swine about the new city site. You are still working on that for us, aren't you, darling?'

'I'm mentioning it whenever I can.'

'Thanks, sweetie.' He leaned over and kissed her cheek. 'Come on, we'll go on with this chat in the office.' He flung a towelling robe over his nakedness, and they walked down together. 'Get my things sent over, Lavinia.' The receptionist stared at Emily, but nodded obediently. Emily tucked her hand into the crook of Gerald's arm, as they took a connecting door between the health club and Gerald's office.

'Right, champagne first!'

There was always a chilled bottle of Dom Perignon or Bollinger available wherever Gerald Montague paused for a rest. Emily thought it extravagant, but enjoyed it none the less. While Gerald dressed, she sipped the wine and tried to decide if she was thrilled or appalled at the thought of meeting Andrew in Gerald's home. 'I suppose I really do need a new dress. . .'

'Good thinking.'

'But I can choose it myself.'

'Darling, OK if not in a hurry — but the guests will be arriving at seven-thirty. Better let Anniekins give you a hand this time.'

'All right. Turn her loose!'

'Quaint expression. I'll just give her a ring.' He pressed the necessary buttons, and summoned Annabel. Then he put the phone down. 'She'll be here in twenty minutes. What shall we do till then?' His eye was roguish. 'Come here, my little blonde bombshell. Your being by my side tonight will make all the difference. It's what I've dreamed of.'

'I know — you did tell me in your letters.'

He enfolded her in his arms. 'Darling, I do love you, you know. You're not the sort of girl one can just blot out of the mind. That six months in London was the highlight of my life.'

'Only to be outdone by getting that city site of Dashwood's?'

'Well — it will come a close second, my sweet.'

Emily laughed. 'You are nice when you're honest, Gerry.'

'Kiss me, Emily.'

She kissed him. She put both arms round his neck and kissed him on the lips. But she felt nothing. Anatomically her mouth and his were in the correct position for pleasure — but nothing happened — no fireworks, no playing of trumpets or pounding of drums. It was just a juxtaposition of mouths, and not a spark resulted. Instead Emily felt a most disloyal feeling, as she found herself longing from the depths of her being for this frog to turn into her handsome Andrew.

Gerald put his hand behind her head, and murmured, 'You can do better than that, Emily.' He bent his head, and his kissing became more urgent. His tongue flickered between her lips, and she found herself at the receiving end of Gerald's pent-up desire. She found his grunting protestations unromantic, and his sweating face pressed against hers unappealing.

He paused, as if aware of his lack of success. 'What are you thinking, darling?'

She brushed her hair back and tried to be practical. 'Gerald, I think you ought to fill me in on what you want me to do tonight. I ought to know just what is expected of me.'

'Be a hostess. Preside at my table and be charming to the guests.'

'That's easy. But ought I to know any danger zones — things I ought not to talk about?'

'Good thinking, sweet. Obviously, no pressure on

Dashwood tonight. Officially it's all very low-key, and no one is putting the screws on—yet. But he knows what I want, and I know he thinks he will never agree. Keep off that subject tonight. Be nice to him.'

Be nice to Andrew? Her feelings about that man were so confused that she wasn't sure if she could control them where he was concerned. But it was her duty to try. She said innocently, 'You were joking, weren't you—about blackmailing him?'

'I'm a businessman, my love. I've learnt the hard way that you keep all your options open. And don't use that word, sweet—it makes it sound so—underhand! All I plan to do is bring up the subject quietly with Dashwood, and let the rest of the fellows see what he has to say for himself.'

'And vote him off the board?'

'It might be arranged later. But I still want to take things softly at present. All to play for, so to speak.' Gerald paused, and then looked across at Emily. A shadow seemed to cross his face and plunge it in darkness. 'All to play for, eh, sweetie? Even you?'

'Gerald, that's not fair.'

'You can't deny he's a good-looking guy.'

'And I work for him—but none of that makes any difference. I came here to see you, Gerald, and to help you. I have all your letters planning our future, and I think you have mine. It's all in the open. That's my style, and we've never been underhand with each other. Let's not lose that.'

He looked down at her, and he curled his lip. It might have been her imagination, but did she see mistrust in his eyes? He repeated, 'As I said, sweetie, be nice to him. It could mean a lot to me.'

'I'll honestly do my best.'

Gerald looked into her wide, sincere eyes, and

seemed repentant at his harsh tone earlier. 'I know you will, love. Emily, you do get under my skin — if I lost you now, I'd never get over it.'

Very conscious of the failure of their last kiss, Emily tried once more, reaching up and kissing his cheek. 'Friends, Gerald?'

'Sure thing. And one of the sexiest friends I've ever had.'

Emily drew herself up, and tried not to be offended by his supposed compliment. Fortunately the doorbell saved her from answering. It was Annabel. 'I've called Felipe, my couturier — he's expecting us, Emily. He has several off-the-peg models, but if you want something specially he'll have it made up for you within the hour.'

Gerald said, 'Is he bringing them here?'

Annabel looked up at him, and Emily was struck forcibly by the understanding and the rapport between them in that single look. She said, 'He'll bring them if we ask him. But I did say I would take Emily downtown. There's so much more to look at there.'

The two women were driven in the Mercedes to the end of Orchard Road. 'Felipe hates doing things on the spur of the moment. He's very artistic, you know. But Gerald has done him a few favours, so no problem. You tell him what you want, Emily, and you'll get it.'

'It must be wonderful to have such power.'

'It's a way of life with Gerald.'

They didn't take long to decide that a dark colour would suit Emily's fair hair. Felipe Casals was enchanted by her figure. 'A slim-fitting shift — that is all we need to bring out your beauty, *señorita*.'

'But with style, Felipe.' Annabel, with her ample curves, was slightly put out by Felipe's praise of the slimmer look. 'We don't want to be vulgar, do we?'

Emily allowed them to argue for a while, but she had

spotted a dress she loved, and waited until they had finished bickering before she announced, 'The blue chiffon, please, Felipe.'

'The blue chiffon!'

'Yes, please. It's simple and neat—and I think the colour suits me.'

'But——' Annabel was distraught at the simplicity of the shirt-waister with its swirling skirt, but Emily wouldn't be moved.

'It's comfortable to wear. No hostess can do her job properly unless she's comfortable.'

When they got back to the apartment, as directed, Gerald was dressing, but he had left some Bollinger '38 in a pail of ice for them. Annabel said, 'I'll go and change.'

'Sorry you don't like my dress.'

'It's lovely, Emily—but with a waist like yours it seems a pity not to make the best of it with a fitted style.'

'I'm a hostess, not a sex symbol.'

'Yes, of course.'

Emily said to her retreating back, 'You'll see, Annabel—guests don't feel comfortable with a hostess who is trying to make an impression. They are happier with someone who thinks they're more important than she is.'

'You could be right.' Annabel's voice betrayed all her irritation with a rival who was younger, prettier and slimmer than herself, and who also said sensible things.

Wearing the dainty blue chiffon, her hair swept up and with sapphires borrowed from Annabel in her ears, Emily sipped champagne with Gerald, and listened to his final words of encouragement. He was saying, 'How I hope this is the start of many happy dinner parties, my darling,' when the doorbell pealed, and the lift was dispatched down to bring up the first guests.

Two portly Chinese colleagues were first, and both showed appreciation of their pretty hostess, teasing Gerald somewhat, and telling each other that having such a stunner sent Gerald up several pegs in their estimation. Annabel was silent, and Emily felt embarrassment for her, knowing that she had been the hostess in the past, and that the guests didn't realise that women had feelings.

When the lift zoomed up the second time, Emily was still thinking of Annabel's feelings, and wishing she could blot out the hurt the previous guests had done. But all thoughts disappeared as Andrew, totally dashing and debonair in a white dinner-jacket, stepped out into the room, carrying a spray of red roses. For a moment they stood, looking at one another, and her heart turned somersaults because he was so crazily handsome and she remembered the damage those gentle lips could cause.

He held out the roses. 'For—for my hostess. Thank you for asking me.'

'It's just a business meeting, Andrew. Nothing personal.'

'The flowers—the flowers are personal. Could I have one for my buttonhole?' She smiled and, taking the bouquet, she broke off a small rosebud with a single leaf, and handed it to him. 'Put it in for me?'

She could feel the heat of his body as she slid the flower through his buttonhole and patted it to keep it in place. 'You do that very well, Emily.'

'Andrew, you're sarcastic. You think I'm one of them, don't you? One of the leeches on the board?'

'Well, aren't you? You're here, in a penthouse,

wearing *haute couture* and drinking champagne as though it were lemonade.'

'You know as well as I do that this isn't the real me.'

'I suppose——' Andrew's voice lowered, and his eyes were expressive. 'I think I've met the other side of you, Emily, but which one is the real one?'

Gerald was coming towards them. Emily only had time to say, 'Don't bother to try to find out. Our paths will only cross at work, and there you won't find me wanting.'

Andrew was already smiling at Gerald, and holding his hand out. His voice was low, his words directed at Emily. 'I wish I could believe you.' Then he looked directly into Gerald's face and greeted him with a hearty indifference. 'Thanks for asking me, Gerald. What's the agenda for this evening?'

'More or less what we went over at the last meeting, but in a more relaxed atmosphere.'

'I think you're deploying your secret weapon, old man.'

'Can't think what you mean, Dashwood. We're all friends here—no need of weapons, surely.' Only Emily realised the hidden menace in those words, and recognised the hooded danger in Gerald's dark eyes. She was called away then, to greet another Chinese businessman, accompanied by the only woman board member, a steel-haired, angular woman with a handshake like a vice. Emily played her part with as much aplomb as she could muster, confident in her appearance, and only afraid that Andrew Dashwood would pierce her sophistication. Only he had the ability to get through to her—and she hoped very much that he didn't know it.

At the table the food was a Chinese eight-course banquet, and chopsticks were used by all, with a revolving section in the centre of the table that spun round so that everyone could help themselves from the tasty morsels heaped high by uniformed waiters. Gerald led the conversation, so that one by one items from the previous meetings were discussed. When it came to Andrew's city block, Gerald skimmed over it. Emily admired his diplomatic skill. 'We all know what the situation is regarding the Haw Sing building. Andrew isn't yet persuaded to let us have it, but I think perhaps in a week or so a higher price might remind him of the fortune to be made, the sooner we get started on the renovations.'

Andrew casually speared an abalone with a chopstick. 'I wish I knew who decided Haw Sing is for sale, because no one told me. It's not available, Montague. Even if I didn't own the lease, it still wouldn't be available.'

The grey-haired woman intervened. 'Dashwood, don't you agree that some of the most successful business ventures happen by accident? Isn't this such a happy accident? Together we all have a chance to make a lot of money. You more than any of us. You know how volatile the markets are — you really would be foolish to let this chance go.'

Andrew sipped his wine, and his eyes looked from one to another around the table, dwelling longest on Emily. She knew she ought not to interrupt, but something inside her responded to Andrew's unspoken plea, and she said quietly, 'From where I sit, I see that Dr Dashwood is very well aware of the money side of the deal. There doesn't seem to be much point in emphasising it again.'

Gerald said swiftly, 'Quite right, Emily, quite right. We're getting nowhere by repeating ourselves. Can we leave this in your court, Dashwood?'

'Whatever you say.' He was offhand about it, but his eyes thanked her for her gentle interruption.

On leaving, Andrew was brief. 'Thank you both. Dinner was superb, and the company just as expected.' And he was gone, with an abrupt handshake to Gerald, and a little bow to Emily.

'Well, I think we made some progress.' Gerald was very pleased with the evening, but Emily felt uncomfortable at sympathising with someone who disliked Gerald, and probably her too. It was hard to have a foot in the enemy's camp.

Annabel had been quiet all evening. Now she came back into the room, looking elegant in her sequinned black suit, and without being asked poured Gerald a large brandy. There was a proprietorial look in her eye. 'I know we made progress, Gerry. Well done, dear.'

So that was what Emily ought to have said. She watched them both, and saw clearly how Annabel hated being assigned a back seat, when she was used to being the leading lady. Emily said quietly, 'I must go. I have work tomorrow.'

'Already?' Gerald had lust in his eye now, and that was even worse because Annabel could read him like a book.

'Yes, already. I'm—glad things went well. I'll keep up the good work if I see Andrew at the hospital.' And as Chang came obediently to her call she turned and said to Annabel, 'Goodnight. Thank you for all your help.' As the lift doors closed, Gerald was still sitting, brandy in hand, like a child suddenly cheated of a sweetmeat. 'Look after him, Annabel.' Somehow she knew she would.

CHAPTER EIGHT

'NURSE FAIRLIE! Nurse Fairlie, come and see me!' Little Kim was sitting up in his bed. 'I go for my operation now.' Emily had just come on duty, and Kim had been waiting for her. 'Aunty Wang and Lennie is coming to see me when I wake up.'

The junior nurse already with Kim laughed, and said, 'Thank goodness you come, Staff Nurse. You wouldn't believe he'd already had his pre-med, would you, lah?'

Kim grinned, showing the gap where one of his front milk teeth was missing, the new one just showing through the gum. 'I wait for Nurse Fairlie!'

Emily sat on his bed and persuaded him to lie back on the pillows. 'And I am here, Kim. I know you will be a good boy for the theatre nurse.'

'But you come to Theatre with me!'

'I'll ask Sister——'

But Sue Brown was already in the doorway. She spoke in a low voice to Emily. 'You'd better go with him, Staff Nurse. Dr Dashwood and Dr Mehtani have discussed his case. He has had so much trauma—having the operation delayed because of the outbreak of infection didn't help, and then his status epilepticus weakened him. They thought there might be signs of an upper motor neurone lesion in slight weakness of his limbs—but operation is the only course now. He's in reasonable physical condition at the moment, and they don't want him upset.'

'Very well, Sister.' Sue was in control, and Emily replied in like manner. It was difficult to tell if Sue had seen Andrew Dashwood over the weekend, because she was being very businesslike and efficient. But last time she had seen them together, Andrew had been comforting Sue after the little argument she had had with Emily.

Emily tried not to think about anything but the operation in hand. 'I'll come with you, Kim.' But he was suddenly drowsy, willing to lie back in his little hospital gown and wait for his bed to be taken down to Theatre. Emily carefully checked his notes, and his wrist nametape, and stroked his brow as he opened his eyes sleepily to make sure she was there, and reached up to hold on to her finger.

The bed was pushed silently along the corridor, and she walked alongside in case he woke again, but, satisfied, the little chap was already confidently facing his ordeal. Emily smiled, as she handed over the notes to the theatre staff. 'Let me know the moment surgery is over, and I'll come for him.'

She walked back to the ward. Dashwood was already sweeping from room to room, his white coat flapping open as usual. She waited demurely out of his view. She didn't want to speak to him unless it was on hospital business. She recalled his stiff little bow as he left her and Gerald after their dinner party. There was little affection there. Sue Brown's jealousy had been making it all up. Yet — when Emily had allowed his kisses, the warmth and enthusiasm in them had belied his cool exterior. He was just one of those men who enjoyed women's company. He would never be tied down. Not to Sue, not to Emily, not to anyone. It would be better not to allow herself to be alone with him again. She knew it might be easy to weaken if he took her in his arms.

'Staff Nurse Fairlie, come along at once. Don't dawdle. There are three patients to be taken to the treatment-room for lumbar puncture.' Sue seemed resolved to keep her busy. 'And don't hang about in the treatment-room. Dr Dashwood has the houseman with him. He'll buzz for you if he needs you. I want you to go round the ward and check everyone's blood tests again.'

'But I thought we'd been cleared of Klebsiella infection — that porter in ICU.'

'Don't answer back, Nurse. You know as well as I do that we must always be vigilant in such cases, having vulnerable patients like children and surgical cases.'

Sue was right, of course — but did she really need to be so harsh? Emily said mildly, 'Is Kim to be nursed in Intensive Care?'

'No, that's where the infection started. Dr Dashwood thinks he would be safer here with barrier nursing.'

'I agree. We know his condition here, and we have more neuro-trained nurses if anything does go wrong.'

Sue snapped, 'No one asked for your approval, Nurse. Here — take these notes and start taking the lumbar punctures down!'

'Yes, Sister.' Sue's businesslike façade was shattered — she obviously wasn't happy about Emily. Perhaps she had heard that Andrew and she had been at the same dinner party. But one look at Sue's acid face and Emily decided that it wasn't a good idea to try to explain anything now. She took the notes, and went to the room of the first patient on the list.

'Mr Fu? Hello, I'm Nurse Fairlie, and I've come to explain what's happening to you this morning.'

'Thank you, Nurse. I've got these headaches, you see, and——'

Emily didn't want Sue shouting at her again, so she cut him short, saying sympathetically, 'I know, Mr Fu. And we're trying to find the cause. Doctor is just going to take a little fluid from your spine. It's a simple test — just a little prick, but we can learn quite a lot about your condition from it. If you wouldn't mind putting this robe on and getting in the wheelchair?'

She bustled about the youngish man, who looked pale and drawn from the pain in his head. She was well aware that all the tests should be done quickly, so that, if clear, he could be reassured that his condition was caused by anxiety and tension. If there was a problem found, and the pressure of the cerebrospinal fluid was raised, then the sooner they operated the better.

Andrew Dashwood was standing in the treatment-room checking his syringes. 'Hello, Emily,' he said, conversationally. 'How did you enjoy meeting the SEAH board? You did look nice, you know.'

Emily looked up briefly into his devastating eyes, knew she couldn't cope with their magnetism and looked down at her patient. 'I've brought Mr Fu, Doctor. Here are his notes. Sister said you wouldn't want me to stay.'

'Ah, Mr Fu.' Andrew was professional at once, as the patient was helped on the treatment couch. 'Nurse, would you mind staying here until someone else comes to relieve you?'

'Oh — yes, very well, Doctor.' She positioned herself at his side, trying not to notice that her body heat increased at his nearness, and the rhythm of her heartbeat thudded in her ears so that she was sure he would hear it. She moved slightly, so that she could be in the patient's line of vision, but Andrew suddenly pulled her back and gave her waist a squeeze, before bending to his task, and rubbing the site of the puncture with antiseptic and local anaesthetic, his eyes demurely concentrating on his task.

As she watched him working, admiration for his skill

and his bedside manner overtook her annoyance at the liberty he took in cuddling her without permission. He was never predictable, and she realised this was part of his fascination. But she had decided that he would not take any more liberties with Emily Fairlie. However handsome he was, he was only playing around, and that was no good reason for allowing him to separate her from her duty to Gerald.

Just then the houseman came in. 'Sorry I'm late, Doctor. The Parkinson patient just passed out in the corridor. I've taken another sample of blood—his temp is raised, and we're just hoping the infection isn't a leftover Klebsiella.'

Emily excused herself. 'I was just going to check the blood results, doctor. Can you do without me now?'

Andrew stood upright for a moment and grinned at her. 'All right, Nurse Fairlie. I'll try and survive!' And she knew he was still smiling as she retreated from the room, blushing hotly.

All the patients had been tested for infection, but Sister—quite rightly—had demanded a second sample just to ensure that the ward was completely clear. The results were through, and Emily's job was to scan all the results and make sure the slips went into the correct folders. She sat patiently going through them, her head bent and her mind absorbed.

Just then she heard the rustle of a white coat, and turned to find Andrew standing behind her. 'Oh, sorry—you wanted your next lumbar puncture patient?'

'No, Emily—I came to ask you a favour.' He wasn't smiling now, and his voice was low and serious. 'Will you come with me after work? I want to show you the Haw Sing building.'

She looked up in surprise. 'I'd like that very much.'

'Good. I'll pick you up at the flat.'

'No—please no.'

'Why ever not?'

'It's—you know—Sue——'

'My dear, I'm not going to be told what to do by a nurse—by any nurse. Be there. I'll pick you up.'

'All right.' It was for Gerald, wasn't it? So it was all right to meet Andrew after work—briefly, just to see the famous building that all the fuss was about.

She went back to her paperwork. All the tests seemed to be clear, but the Parkinson patient had been admitted on the day of the repeat tests, and his present result was not yet to hand. Just then there was a buzz, and she knew it must be Andrew ready for the next patient in the treatment-room. She put the remaining forms in a neat pile, and went to bring Mr Fu back and collect the next.

Andrew said nothing when she went in, except, 'I think I've got an Indian gentleman next—a Mr Jahan.' She was pushing the wheelchair back and looking out for the room where Mr Jahan would be, when Sue came after her, her face stony.

'One of my nurses has had to go up to assist in Gynae. I'm afraid I need you to stay on for three hours after six this evening.'

'But——'

'I'm sorry if you have a date.' The inflexion was obvious. She must have seen or heard them making their arrangement.

'It isn't that—don't I get a break for tea?'

'Naturally.'

'Thanks. I'll be there.' Emily went into the room to get Mr Jahan ready, taking no more notice of Sue. But it was disappointing all the same. It would have been interesting to get to the bottom of the Haw Sing case, and find the reason why Andrew wouldn't sell.

There was no opportunity to tell Andrew she couldn't meet him. Sue Brown hovered like a vulture in blue, making sure Emily was worked hard, with tasks waiting to be done, while Andrew was busy in the treatment-room. The clock ticked round to lunchtime, and then she was sent to Recovery to look after Kim. He was very drowsy, but Dr Mehtani was pleased. 'I am glad you have come to stay with him, Nurse Fairlie—he speaks of you with such affection.'

'What did you find, Doctor?'

The surgeon's eyes clouded. 'We were almost too late. In fact, if I had not operated today, there might have been damage to his eyesight. The cortical veins were thrombosing.'

'Nothing malignant?' Emily's own eyes opened wide at what the little fellow had just avoided.

'Nothing malignant. Scar tissue from birth trauma, at a guess. I've anastomosed the veins, and with a little help from the Almighty he should make a complete recovery—and should have no more fits. But don't say anything to his relatives yet—it's not over for at least a month, so keep him calm at all times, and I'll come and write him up for antibiotics and anticoagulants.'

'That's marvellous news.' But Emily looked sad. 'His relative couldn't get here. But, thank goodness, his old roommate, Lennie Wang, will be in at two with his mother.'

'You think of everything, Nurse Fairlie. I think we are very lucky to have poached you from the Royal Lester.'

'That's very kind, sir.'

Mehtani smiled and nodded, and then proceeded to beckon his theatre sister for a new mask and gown. 'I'll see you in the ward, Nurse.'

Emily went back to Recovery, but young Kim was

very sleepy, and she had little to do for a couple of hours but sit calmly by the bed, and ponder on how her life in Singapore was turning out. She loved the work — but not her ward sister. She knew she had fallen for Dr Dashwood's crinkly blue eyes and deep velvet voice. But she also knew that he was a man alone, a man no woman could tame, and, as such, she wasn't going to waste time pining for him. All the same, she had her promise to Gerald to keep, and that promise consisted of sticking by Andrew whenever he was on South East Asia Health Clubs business. Pity she wasn't free to meet him tonight. It would have been great finally to get a glimpse of the Haw Sing building, and see what all the fuss was about. She sighed.

When she finally walked back to the ward with Kim, it was after two, and she was feeling rather hungry. But Lennie and his mother were waiting, and Emily thought it wasn't breaking a confidence to tell Mrs Wang that the operation had gone according to plan. 'I'm so happy for the little child. Tell me, Nurse, when does he have to go back to that lonely big house he was telling Lennie about?'

'A couple of weeks at least.'

'Time to make some enquiries about him staying with Lennie from time to time?' the kindly soul asked, with the glow of compassion in her almond eyes.

'Mrs Wang, that would be wonderful.'

There was a sudden interruption, an unfriendly voice that had dogged Emily all day. Sister Brown had stuck her head round the door. 'There's a telephone call for you, Staff Nurse Fairlie. I hope you will tell whoever it is that personal calls are not allowed on duty.'

'I'm not expecting —'

'Oh, hurry up and get him off the line, Nurse!'

She went to the office, and picked up the receiver

that had been left lying on the desk. 'Hello? Nurse Fairlie?'

'Emily, sweetie, thank goodness that old coot allowed me to speak to you. Who does she think she is, anyway?'

'Well, dear, she is in charge of a ward full of seriously ill patients. What can I do for you that couldn't wait?'

'You sound almost as grumpy as her, Em. But it's an emergency — I need you to step in and turn on the old charm tonight. I know it's short notice, but this guy from Bangkok is going to be in town tonight, and he wants to take us out for a meal. Can you put on the old gladrags again and be here for eight?'

The man Gerald went to see in Thailand — the one who had the dirt on Andrew — wanted to blackmail him! 'I'm sorry, Gerald. I'm working until ten.'

'Ten! Good God, woman, what do they think you are, a bloody cart-horse? Can't you tell them you have a business engagement?'

She resented his high-handed approach. But then, he had always resented her work taking her away from him, even in London. 'Nursing isn't a business, Gerry, it's a way of life. I could leave a business in the lurch, but I can't leave my patients, I'm afraid. Sorry.'

'I knew this would crop up as soon as you said you wanted to work!' His voice was rising. Gerald hated to be refused anything.

Emily said coolly, 'In fact, work has been the best part of Singapore so far. I'm so glad I can lose myself in it.'

There was a telling silence. Then he said, 'You are living at second hand — using other people's troubles as a substitute for real life.'

'Oh, no, Gerald — it's the opposite. Your life is something of a fantasy. I live in the real world. And I meet some wonderful people in it too.'

'No doubt you mean Dashwood?' Gerald's voice sounded petty suddenly.

'His name never entered my head—I'm talking of two little friends, and a mother who has found room in her heart and her home for a lonely little boy. Goodbye, Gerald. I'll call you tomorrow. I hope the evening goes well.'

There was no answer, and Emily put the phone down before Gerald did. She could imagine him now, frowning and drumming his fingers on the table before reaching for his glass of champagne. But Annabel would be there. Annabel always made him feel better. All the same, Emily was sorry for letting him down. Because she wasn't free anyway—she had promised to go to the Haw Sing building with Andrew. Tonight she could take up neither man's invitation—and all because of Sue Brown's jealousy.

She turned on her heel and went back to her duties. Dr Dashwood was in the treatment-room speaking with Sue Brown, so Emily quickly backed away before she was seen. But she heard him saying, 'It sounds a great idea, Sue, but not tonight. I'm—otherwise engaged tonight.'

'Not with Emily Fairlie, you aren't—I need her to work late. Clementina has gone to help out in Gynae—they're short-staffed.'

His voice sounded suspicious. 'Did you suggest sending Clementina on purpose, Sue?'

'No. How could you speak to me like that? They requested her!'

'OK, OK, sorry. I do know how good a sister you are—I've had many a case success to prove it. Say, let's make tomorrow definite, shall we? Just like the old days?'

Emily turned away, trying not to be dejected at the

thought of Sue and Andrew making a date, sounding happy together. After all, it should considerably improve Sue's mood. She went back to see Kim, but he was fast asleep, with a model aeroplane clutched in his hand. She detached it and placed it on his locker, her training automatically removing anything from an epileptic boy that might hurt him. She looked longingly at a sliver of chocolate overlooked accidentally that had been left by the bed. She had missed lunch, and it was now nearly teatime. She waited until Sue came back — Sue's eyes a lot brighter than they were that morning — and made a humble request to take half an hour off to get something to eat.

'You haven't eaten?'

'No — I was sitting with Kim in Recovery.'

'Then go along at once. I don't want you flaking out on me.'

'Thanks, Sister.'

'But make an effort to be back by five, Nurse. I'll be going off at six, and I want to make sure you know what to do.'

'Yes, Sister.' Sue was deliberately treating Emily like a learner, even though Emily's qualifications were better than Sue's, and she had run a department three times the size of the Ambassador Clinic single-handed. It was all a matter of patience. Once Sue realised that Emily was no rival, she was sure they would get on like real colleagues. Jealousy was a nasty thing when taken to extreme, as Sue was doing so blatantly.

When she returned from the dining-room after snatching a cup of tea and a curry puff, she noticed that Andrew was leaving by the front exit. Sue had manipulated them both very cleverly that day, keeping them apart and now making sure that they did not say goodbye. Shrugging her shoulders, Emily took a deep breath, told herself to be very sensible and not start a row, and tapped on Sue's door.

Sister Brown swung round in her chair. Her face was a lot happier now — almost triumphant. 'Here's the duty list. I'm still worried about Mr Fu, even though his CSF was clear and normal pressure. Keep an eye on him every half-hour or so.' She handed the list of patients — and Emily refrained from telling her that she would have checked on these patients anyway, as a matter of course, and as part of good nursing.

'I'll see to it.'

'Oh, and Nurse — I want old Mrs Alfonso accompanied to the home.'

'What home is that?'

'It's the hospice in the next block. You get the doorman to order a small ambulance — the driver knows what to do, and see that she is made comfortable and her luggage is unpacked before the ambulance brings you back.'

'What time will that be?'

'They're expecting her at ten. Your relief will be here at nine-thirty.'

'You want me to go with her and not the relief?'

'She has taken a fancy to you. I think you'd be best.'

'OK — you're the boss.'

There was a silence between the two nurses, as Sue realised just how bossy she had been, and Emily waited to see if Sue would thank her for stepping in to do the locum. She didn't. But she did say, 'I've already entered you on the time sheet — it will be double the pay this week.'

Emily nodded, and took the duty list carefully. She ticked off the patients as she saw to them, and by the time Mrs Alfonso was wheeled to the ambulance Emily's eyes were closing with weariness, and her stomach felt as though she had spent a week in the Sahara.

She was interested to see what sort of hospice the clinic sent their patients to. In spite of her tiredness and dragging feet, she looked up at the name over the door as the cheerful Malay driver wheeled the chair up the ramp. Then Emily's eyes jerked open, and her weariness vanished, as she read, 'The Haw Sing Centre'. Pulses racing now, she hurried after the driver and Mrs Alfonso, carrying the little bag of luggage and looking all around her as they trundled along a clean tiled floor towards an archway of light. 'What is this place?' she asked the ambulance driver. 'It doesn't look very luxurious.'

'No—is where people come when they no more money.'

'Is it run by the government?'

'No—on charity, by businessman.'

'He must be a millionaire.'

'Sure thing he must, lah.'

And then they had passed through the archway and into a small lounge, where elderly and frail residents were being taken to bed one by one. And leaning over one who was almost ready to go was the rangy, lean figure of Andrew Dashwood. He was sounding her chest with a stethoscope, and joking with her at the same time. His figure looked lithe and attractive, in close-fitting trousers and neat short-sleeved shirt, showing off his slim waist and broad masculine shoulders. As the old lady was wheeled away by a white-uniformed attendant, he turned and held out his hands to Mrs Alfonso. 'Right on time! Glad to welcome you, my dear!' His face shone with genuine kindness, and he spoke as he might have spoken to a great lady.

Tears suddenly blurred Emily's view. Andrew shook

hands with Mrs Alfonso and called an attendant to see to her, while he himself reached out to take the luggage from Emily. Then he saw who she was, and they both stopped and looked into one another's eyes. A smile brightened his eyes, but didn't reach his lips. 'You made it, then.'

'Sue sent me.'

'I wonder if she knew just what she was doing?' Then he smiled his famous grin that lit up his entire face. 'Well, Nurse Fairlie—now that you're here, let me show you round the Haw Sing Centre.' And he held out his hand, gesturing for her to precede him.

It was sparsely but adequately furnished. There were no carpets on the floors, but that was just as well, because the air-conditioning wasn't very modern, and the rooms were hot. However, wherever he went Andrew was greeted with smiles and blessings, and Emily's tears were never far away.

When all the residents were asleep, and the place had fallen quiet, Andrew turned to her, and she tried not to show her red eyes. He said, 'Well, what do you think?'

'It's a surprise.'

'Shall I turn all these people out so that your Gerald can make a rich folks' health club?'

'It would be sad, Andrew, very sad. But—well couldn't you buy another place? These people don't mind where they are cared for—as long as they have care.'

'It wouldn't be the same. It's a matter of principle. Here they have the shops as well. They look after themselves as much as possible. They are known in the cafés, the post office, the bank, the little cinema. It's like a little village in here. The rich can go anywhere— why shouldn't my people have a tiny share of the city centre, where most of them grew up, and where they are treated as friends and neighbours by everyone?'

'Doctor!' A gentle but troubled voice from one of the rooms, where a nurse was saying, 'I'm afraid it's a stroke. A bad one.'

Andrew went to the patient at once, followed by Emily. He said, 'I can't say I wasn't expecting this. She's almost a hundred.' They worked together to maintain a clear airway and make the patient comfortable in her unconsciousness, placing a soft pad beneath her, and passing an intragastric tube for feeding her.

It was very late when Andrew drove her home. The sky sparkled with stars. He tilted her face up to his, and kissed her very gently. 'Goodnight, little Emily.'

She watched him stride back to his car, wishing he had wanted to stay. 'Goodnight. You —— ?'

He turned. 'My dear, don't.'

'Don't what?'

'Talk to me in that lovely sad voice. You know I want to kiss you, and it wouldn't take much to make me. But I can see just how whacked you are, and I'd be cruel to keep you awake another second longer.'

Emily realised just how much under his spell she was. This was a man she had decided never to be alone with. Yet he had read her thoughts. 'Andrew, go home. And don't interpret things in my voice that certainly are not there! Emily Fairlie might just be the one woman who can withstand your boyish charms. Remember that. But for God's sake don't take it as a challenge.' She was proud of that last sally. But suddenly, as Andrew left, the stars seemed to disappear.

CHAPTER NINE

EMILY awoke slowly, knowing that at last she had caught up with her sleep. She felt wonderful. And today she was off duty. Even Sue Brown couldn't spoil her day. She had seen Andrew Dashwood off with a killing put-down. And Gerald — well, she would phone Gerald just as soon as she was ready, and not before. After all, she wasn't sure now about that Haw Sing Centre. She could see both sides of the argument now, and, being a nurse, could understand Andrew's point of view a little better than Gerald's.

'Gosh, I'm hungry!' She rolled out of bed, visions of hot buttered toast and scrambled eggs being the best things in the world.

'Good!'

Thinking herself back in dreamland, Emily sat on the floor, wondering why she was wearing bra and briefs in bed. Then realisation flooded over her. That word had been spoken by a real person. And that real person was there in her flat, had made breakfast for her, and was sitting there right now.

From her position on the floor, she looked over at Andrew, who was looking bright and alert, and had somehow managed to shave. 'You stayed here all night!'

He smiled, and indicated the breakfast tray. 'You passed out. Will you please do something about your low blood-sugar level before I force-feed you?'

She obeyed, first modestly pulling on her housecoat, although she realised it must have been Andrew who had undressed her last night. She replied, between delicious mouthfuls, 'I had nothing yesterday but a curry puff and a cup of tea.'

'I knew that when you flaked out. Emily, you're still not acclimatised. After all, you spend most of your time in air-conditioning. When you go out in the Singapore air, and you haven't eaten, the heat gets to you. When are you going to realise this? Sue Brown might be a slave-driver, but she doesn't want a useless member of staff, does she? Stand up for yourself next time. Just because she's a jealous cat, it doesn't mean she can starve you into relinquishing your claim to my attention.'

'Now just a minute!' Her hunger appeased, Emily laid down her knife and fork. 'Let's be honest about this. I'm not laying any claim on you. You are just someone I work with. After what you showed me last night, I have a lot more respect for you than I did before. But your lady-friends are your business. I ask nothing from you, so you can keep your date with Sue tonight with a clear conscience.'

He smiled, that infuriating slow smile that started at the corners of his eyes, and slowly lit up his entire face. 'Of course. You heard us in the treatment-room. Well done, Emily. You're as wily as Sue!'

'Don't link my name with hers, please. I overheard accidentally, and I was very pleased, because I don't like the way you treat Sue. She deserves better from you.'

Had she hit a nerve? Andrew stood up suddenly, and walked to the window, his hands thrust deep in his pockets. Speaking to the sunlit garden, he said, 'Sue Brown knew from the start that I had no intention of being a couple with anyone. I make my own friends, and no one is going to tell me which of my friends I see—as and when I want to.'

'Maybe some girls aren't as open-minded as you would like them to be?'

He turned round slowly. 'Would you be so possessive, Emily, if you were Sue?'

She had to think about that one, but she was flattered to be asked her opinion. 'I'd try not to be, because I can see that's exactly the sort of behaviour that turns you off. But I would damn well feel it. I'd just be less honest in letting you see it.'

He nodded. 'Thanks for that. I'll see her tonight,' he said shortly.

'Good.'

He stood for a while, head down, thinking. Emily began to hate herself. 'Andrew—I only answered your questions. I'm not trying to put you down. I work with Sue, remember? I can see how unhappy she is.'

'That's just what I didn't want. I never wanted anyone to rely on me for their happiness.'

For the first time Andrew Dashwood seemed to want to talk about himself. Emily dared to ask a question. 'Is that—because you're committed to your work?'

With shadowed eyes, he replied shortly, 'In a way.'

Emily kept up gentle pressure to talk. 'The upkeep of that centre must be enormous.'

'The rents from the shops and offices help. But yes, it takes a lot of my income.'

Emily said slowly, 'And do you intend to live without personal commitment for the rest of your life?'

'It's easier.' He paused, and looked back at her. 'I've sown my wild oats—a long time ago.'

'Oh, God—the man from Bangkok!' He had admitted his past indiscretion to her, and she was shocked by the simplicity of his admission. The words of surprise just slipped out.

He took his hands from his pockets and strode towards her as she sat at the table, her robe falling loosely about her. 'How could you possibly know that?'

'I don't know anything about it. But Andrew—I do know that the man from Bangkok has some information that Gerald is hoping to use to—persuade you—to sell the Centre to SEAH. It just occurred to me that your wild oats might have something to do with that.'

'Oh, God.' He stood very silently, close to her, and after a while she reached out and took his hand. Absent-mindedly, he moved closer to her and put his arms around her shoulders, so that her cheek was resting against his hard, flat stomach. Emily felt herself grow warm at his physical closeness, and allowing her arms to encircle his body, feel the firmness of his rounded buttocks and long, lean back.

For a long time they remained linked together in proximity and in sympathy. Then slowly he drew her up into his arms, and their embrace became more passionate. He sought and found her lips, and she knew she had been hoping for this, her body glowingly ready for this intimacy.

He kissed her for a long time, their mouths eager for each other, their lips growing swollen and electrified by the other's closeness and desirability. Her robe was open, and her body pressed against him so that she was aware of the depths of his need. It was unfair to push him away, but at the back of her mind she knew that falling for Andrew Dashwood wasn't going to solve her dilemma of what to do with her life. Gathering her resolve from the depths of pleasure wasn't easy, but she managed to murmur, 'Don't take on another dependent female, Andrew. Get out now before we do something we'll regret.'

He took his arms away, but let his hands fall gently down her arms, pausing at her breasts to touch the tips, and sense just how aroused she was. He groaned, 'Oh, Emily, Emily——' then he took a step backwards. 'Thank you for telling me.'

'About the blackmail?'

'Yes.'

She moved away to sit on the dining chair. 'What are you going to do?'

He smoothed back his hair wearily. 'Go away and think.'

She said, not expecting an answer, 'What happened in Bangkok?'

His eyes blazed with sincerity then, and he caught her hands in his. 'Nothing I'm ashamed of, Emily. You've got to believe that. Nothing ignoble. Nothing anyone would care about — except that the person concerned was — not free to give herself to me. I didn't know that. But I swore never to tell anyone, and her reputation was saved.' He let her hands go, and said miserably, 'I had no idea anyone else knew. I've said too much already. I'd better go.' And she looked up at him, feeling every ounce of his personal misery in her own tender heart.

Then the telephone shrilled into their consciousness, driving them apart. 'Emily!' It was Gerald, and his voice was sharp, agitated. She had never heard him so upset.

'Yes, Gerald? I was going to call you later.'

'It's important — something you might be able to help us with through your hospital work.'

'Go on. I'll help if I can.'

'It's Annabel. She's had an appalling headache all

night. Not the usual migraine — much worse. Tablets wouldn't touch it last night. It's easing off now, but I'm very worried, Emily.'

'She should see her doctor at once. Call him out, Gerald!'

'She won't let me. She's scared of — a brain haemorrhage, I suppose. Oh Em, what shall I do?'

'OK, listen carefully. If she's able, get her to an ophthalmologist right away. That way she'll think it's a sight problem.'

'And isn't it?'

'A good eye examination can tell a doctor a lot. Ask the ophthalmologist to phone Andrew immediately with the results, and bring her along yourself or get someone to come with her.'

'Andrew! Why him?'

'Because he's a damn good doctor, that's why. If there's anything seriously wrong, he's the one to arrange further tests and treatment.'

He said anxiously, 'I'll do it.' Emily slowly put the phone back.

Andrew looked expectant. 'What was all that? Who's ill?'

'Annabel.' Emily described the symptoms. 'Did I do right?'

'Yes, I suppose you did, but an ophthalmologist might not diagnose a haemorrhage until it's too late. Will they contact me?'

'Yes. And he was going to take her at once.' She managed an ironic smile. 'You're just about to give help and advice to the man who is going to blackmail you.'

Andrew's good humour had returned. He shrugged and smiled. 'That's medicine for you.'

Emily said, 'I'd better go round and see if there's

anything I can do.' She looked into Andrew's face, and tried not to love him. 'I'm going to try to make them drop the Haw Sing project. I'll probably fail, but I'll make a damn good case for leaving it alone.'

He nodded. 'Not many little people can fight big business. But thanks for being nearly on my side.' He drew her into his arms again, and they kissed warmly, sweetly, but without menacing passion—like good friends. He held her longer in his arms, and she was content just to lean against him, knowing how alone she would feel when he went away.

She watched him walk away along the path, those long legs covering the distance quickly. He didn't look back. That's just Andrew, she thought. No commitments. And tonight he was meeting Sue. She must stop allowing these fanciful ideas about taming him to dominate her thoughts. Andrew had had his fingers burned in Thailand. Now he was a loner, and especially now that the threat of blackmail hung over him it was impossible for him ever to trust a relationship again.

Emily called Gerald, but the butler said he was out, and she knew he must have taken Annabel to the ophthalmologist. On the off-chance, she made her way to the Tanglin Palace, where Gerald's office was next to the health club. He was there, biting his nails and sipping champagne. 'Emily, am I glad to see you, pet!'

'How is Annabel?'

'Already gone to the Ambassador, thanks to you. The eye chappie told me there was something abnormal pressing on the back of the eye. I didn't tell Annabel, but he advised her very tactfully to have a CT scan, and she's gone down there now with Mrs Scott—the grey-haired lady on our board. I feel sorry for old Anniekins. She's been a brick to me.'

'I know.' Emily wondered if he knew just how much devotion had been lavished on him by the faithful Annabel. 'Tell me, has she had any other symptoms?'

'She's been forgetful lately. I thought——' he smiled modestly '—I thought she was jealous because you've come into my life, and you're so decorative and young and pretty compared with her.'

'Rubbish! She's terribly attractive, Gerald. And superbly dressed. If only she hadn't dyed her hair to please you.'

Gerald looked puzzled for a moment. Then he saw the point. 'I've gone on about blondes, I suppose. Oh, well, it wasn't jealousy, was it? There must be something else. Oh, God, Emily, I do hope she doesn't have a tumour.'

'Dr Mehtani can help.'

'I thought you said Andrew would help.'

'Andrew is the diagnostician. He sees to the tests. Mehtani is the surgeon. They work together. Don't worry. If this is the first headache she's had, then it can't be too serious.' But Emily knew she was being over-confident for the sake of Gerald. She had seen some people with bad tumours who had no symptoms at all. She crossed her fingers, and prayed silently.

But when she went into work the next day, Annabel was awaiting surgery. Without make-up, and with tear stains on her cheeks, she looked very vulnerable. 'They say it's not malignant, Emily. How on earth can they possibly know until they look?'

'All sorts of ways.'

'But it's—growing inside my head!'

'Only the way a little wart grows on your finger— once it's out, then there'll be no more trouble, honestly.'

'I wish I could believe you.'

At that moment Andrew came into the room with some X-rays. He looked at Emily, and gave a little nod of understanding. She felt a rush of closeness, of intimacy. She knew him now, so well, present and past, and the more she knew, the more she liked. But because it was useless she was going to try very hard not to let it show.

Annabel said, 'Are those of my head, Andrew?'

'They are, yes. I thought you'd like to see — just a small growth, which Dr Mehtani will be able to remove quite easily, because it's in an accessible place.'

'Will — my hair be shaved?'

'Yes, it will have to be. But we have a lovely selection of wigs until your own hair comes back. And often it comes back even lovelier and more luxuriant than before.'

'You're very comforting, Andrew. Are there any more tests to do?'

'I'm afraid one more. An angiogram. Your surgeon must be able to plan his operation so as to miss any major blood vessels. This test will show them up. I'll do it under a small general anaesthetic, so you won't feel any discomfort.'

'I've been in a daze ever since that headache. I'm glad it's going to be over soon.'

'You'll find your thinking has become a bit muzzy, Annabel. The moment you wake you'll know that things are back to normal, I promise.'

Annabel looked up at him, and said sincerely, 'We've — had some words in the past, Andrew. I hope you don't think——'

'I don't want to hear anything about the outside world, my dear, until you're fit and capable of coping with it again.'

'You're a kind person. I do appreciate it.'

'I hope you still think so after the angiogram! Bring her along in twenty minutes, Emily. I have to get the new dye first.'

Sister Brown was late on duty. Emily noted that she was in a good humour. That meant that last night she and Andrew had. . . Emily didn't want to think about it. Ruefully she realised it was she who was the jealous one now, and she strove manfully to stop her hurt feelings from getting the better of her caring nature.

Dr Mehtani was down in the ward, visiting his patients, and writing up prescriptions for them. He spotted Emily. 'You must be worried. Miss Annabel tells me you are a friend of hers.'

'She does? I appreciate it.' It must have been hard for Annabel to accept Emily at all, even less call her a friend, when she had arrived in Singapore to turn Annabel's little world upside-down by taking away the man she loved. 'She has always been very kind to me.'

'Well, by your rapid diagnosis, Emily, you have done her a very good turn.'

'I have? I thought it was only a tiny benign tumour.'

'Yes, but very close to the optic nerve. As it is, I can save her sight. Another month or two, and the nerve would have had to be severed to remove the growth.'

'Do me a favour, Doctor, and don't tell her that!'

'To be sure I won't. Some medical details are best forgotten, providing all goes well.'

Gerald came in that evening with a bunch of red roses in his hand. Emily realised that it might be an awkward meeting, to see him giving red roses to Annabel with his fiancée looking on. So she asked Sue if she could go off duty a few minutes early.

'Of course. Thanks, Emily, for a good day's work.'

'Don't mention it.' The very sight of Sue's good humour made Emily recall the reason for it. Andrew

Dashwood's charm had worked again, and made another lady very happy. As Emily ambled across to her bungalow she wondered again about the lady in Bangkok whom Andrew had loved. Was she very high up in the land? In politics? Did her husband perhaps stride the world's stage as a diplomat or government official? Whoever it was, Emily was sure she remembered Andrew with affection even now. He was a gentleman through and through. He didn't deserve the hard time Gerald and his board were giving him. Would this episode of Annabel's illness perhaps soften Gerald's ambitions to acquire the Haw Sing?

'Emily!' She heard his voice behind her, and knew that yet again he had watched her go, and caught her up just at that point in the path where the rustic seat was hidden from both hospital and residences. 'Don't run away from me.'

'Have we anything to talk about?' she smiled.

He sat down and reached up to pull her down beside him. 'I'll think of something.'

'I'd really like to get back. I need to rest if Annabel is having surgery tomorrow. I promised to stay with her even though I'm off. It's a half-day.'

'Well, there was something I wanted.'

'OK, you've got it.'

He smiled lazily, and she knew she had agreed too readily. 'I wanted to sit and look at you. It's been a hard day for me, too. I like something bright, cool and beautiful to end my day. That to me spells Emily Fairlie.'

She felt her heart churning. Oh, no, not again. It would be so easy to let him come home with her. But she knew how hurt she would be afterwards. 'Just this once, let me go home by myself? I know you could pull rank or something and force me to invite you in—but I'd like to spend this evening alone.'

He appraised her then, tilting his head back with a half-smile, so that he made her blush. It was a good job the evening was closing in, the crickets starting their nightly chorus, and the moon glowing between the palm trees. 'Well said, Emily. I've never heard anyone lie quite so prettily!'

She didn't answer. He knew damn well it was a lie. He knew how much she wanted him. This man knew all there was to know about women. She waited, almost breathlessly, for his arm to creep around her shoulders. But it didn't. He sat quite still for a moment, listening to the crickets and the squeak of the geckos in the shrubbery. Then he stood up. 'Goodnight, my dear.' She watched helplessly as he merged into the darkness round the corner of the hibiscus hedge, and her heart yearned after him.

I'll never do that again. It's just so awful when a man obeys you! Emily thought, and smiled at herself. 'I'm glad really! she said aloud, stood up, and walked slowly home.

The telephone was ringing as she came in, and she slammed the door before going to pick it up. 'Yes?'

'You're a lying snake, Emily Fairlie!'

'Sue, what is it now?'

'You've got that man with you, and I think it's despicable. You just can't leave him alone, can you? I have a hard enough job getting him to come to supper at my place, yet you grab him every night along that path. You could get any man you wanted! Why do you have to pick on mine? I hate you, Emily. I can never take to you after what you've done to me.'

'He isn't here, Sue.' Emily had to shout to get the other woman to hear through her anger.

'Where is he, then?'

'I don't know. I don't even know where he lives. Is he at the Haw Sing Centre? Isn't that where he goes at night? I've no idea.'

'I'll go and see——'

'Sue, you'll chase him away if you follow him.'

'I've known him a lot longer than you. Just keep your nose out of my business—and my life!' And the phone was slammed down.

It was a petty little affair, but Emily sat for a very long time in the darkness, wondering just why she wanted to stay in this hospital. The work was fascinating, but to have to endure such irrational abuse was upsetting. Perhaps she would be better trying to be Gerald's hostess. Getting involved in business wouldn't be as compassionate as nursing, but she would be using her brains, and hopefully being useful.

Making up her mind, she ate a hasty supper, and then walked back along the path to see if Gerald was still with Annabel. Annabel was alone in her room, her hair dishevelled over the pillow, and tears streaking her cheeks. 'Annabel? Are you awake?' Emily took a step into the room.

Annabel rolled her head on the pillow. 'Oh, it's you, Emily.'

'Gerald gone home?'

'Yes.'

'I'm sure he'll be back to see you tomorrow after surgery.'

With listless voice, Annabel said, 'I don't know.'

'Don't be upset. It isn't the thought of the operation that's bothering you, is it?'

Annabel choked back a sob. 'No, it's you, Emily. Forgive me, but things were going so well before you came. Now everything seems to have gone wrong. Oh,

I don't say I'm not grateful—you've been so sweet to me. You haven't done anything—except just—take Gerald away from me.' And the tears flowed.

Emily stood for a moment, appalled to see the other woman's distress. Then she turned and walked silently from the room. Back in her flat she poured herself some diet lemonade, and wished she had some of Gerald's champagne at that moment. But Annabel was quite right—Emily had walked into Gerald's life and—even though he had invited her—it was really plain that she didn't belong. However hard she tried to pretend, she would never feel at home in that artificial and money-orientated society.

'I seem to have done nothing but offend people. And fall for the wrong man,' she said out loud. She took a deep breath and made up her mind. She would finish her contract at the Ambassador, and then go back to London. It was as simple as that. The only thing she would miss in the whole of Singapore would be Andrew Dashwood—and she had intended to stay away from him anyway, so going back to England was obviously the only thing to do.

She felt happier after making up her mind. 'And I know two unhappy women who will be delighted to hear my news! So now everyone's pleased!'

CHAPTER TEN

ROUTINE work was easier, now that Emily had decided to leave Singapore for good. She felt calm and assured, as she went round the next few days, changing dressings and comforting relatives. Kim was ready for home, and his grandmother was coming to fetch him. The nurses were all agog to see this rich grandmother who had so little time that she never visited her grandson.

Emily chatted to the boy briefly, as she gave him a mirror to see his new hair already beginning to grow. 'Almost as much length in your hair as in your new front tooth, Kim,' she joked.

'Will you come and see me?'

'Promise. And I'll be here when you come for your check-up, Kim. And you'll be seeing Lennie, won't you? You have his phone number?'

'Yes, lah. I write it in my book!'

Someone came in then, and Kim looked up and smiled uncertainly. It was a small, very old, very aristocratic Chinese lady, dressed from head to foot in silver-grey silk, even to the tiny slippers on her feet, and she rustled as she walked — erect, even at her age.

There was a servant running anxiously behind her, and as soon as she stopped a crimson silk-topped stool was placed for her to sit down. She looked at the boy, and the ivory face creased into an answering smile. 'You are better, Kim?'

'Yes, Grandmama.'

'And this lady?'

'This is Emily, Grandmama. She look after me all the time.'

The old lady turned her head, which glistened with diamond and pearl clips and earrings. 'I am grateful to you, Miss Emily. I am not as mobile as I was, but I was assured that my grandson was being well cared-for.'

'He was a delight to care for. And we were lucky that the other boy with him was very nice — as was his mother, Mrs Wang. We're obviously all very pleased that his surgery was a complete success.'

'I will make sure that you are rewarded.'

'No — please. That's not necessary. We did our job, that's all. Sister Brown did as much if not more than I.'

The old lady beckoned to the servant, who handed her a small embroidered purse. She took out a gilt-edged card. 'This is my address. I would like you to come for dinner with Kim and myself one day.'

'Thank you. I'd love to see him again.'

The old lady looked keenly at Emily, and there was a mysteriously knowing smile on the parchment face. 'And I will make sure your Sister Brown is suitably rewarded.' She clapped her hands, and two men came running in from the corridor. One lifted Kim bodily in his arms, while the other collected his things. Emily watched as the regal retinue made its stately departure.

'Wow!' Emily walked back to the office, just in time to see Sue Brown opening a gold box and taking out a diamond ring. It winked and shone with fire in the sunlight through the blinds. Sue said nothing — she hadn't said anything to Emily apart from work — but the hardness in her face had definitely softened. Someone else asked Emily if the old lady had given her anything, and Emily was relieved that she could honestly shake her head. 'But what an exit. She must be very wealthy.'

'She owns half of Pasir Ris,' replied another junior.

'That's enough gossip. Go and tidy the beds!' And Sue wrapped up the box tenderly and put it in her pocket.

Emily was still in the detached mood after her momentous decision to go home, so she saw the Ambassador Clinic as just one phase in her life, and a phase which would be coming to an end before too long. All the same, she felt a secret delight that little Kim would be all right, and also that Mr Fu had been given the all-clear, and had been discharged on mild tranquillisers. Even detached people like Emily wanted to be sure that the people they cared about were happy. . . Now all that remained today was to go and see Annabel in Recovery, and tell her the good news that Emily wouldn't be on the scene much longer.

Annabel looked relaxed and lazy, a bandage swathed round her head. 'Dr Mehtani is very pleased.'

'I'm glad, Annabel. Is there anything I can get you?'

'No — I'm just so happy it's all over.'

'So am I. Thank goodness it was straightforward.'

Annabel held out her hand. 'Emily, I know I was awfully rude to you the other night. I wasn't thinking straight. I want to thank you with all my heart for getting me seen to so quickly. I overheard the surgeons as I was coming round discussing what they would have had to do if my optic nerve had been affected.'

'That's OK, Annabel. All over now.'

Annabel clung to her hand. 'I do apologise. I'm happy for you to be here. I don't know what came over me. Please say it's all right.'

'Of course it's all right.' Emily looked at her, wanting her to know the truth. 'But you did talk sense, and it made me rethink what I am really doing here. We both know now that I'm not suitable for Gerald. I expect he realises it, but is too embarrassed to tell me to my face. So, Annabel—I've made up my mind—I'm going to see him this evening to make it clear that I won't be staying on after my six months at the Ambassador is up.'

'He'll be so angry with me——'

Emily reassured her, trying to show this good-hearted soul that she had done nothing wrong, 'I won't mention you. It's all my own idea.' And Emily bent and kissed Annabel's cheek.

Emily sat alone in the dining-room at lunchtime. Mai Li was on holiday, and the others were busy. She was grateful in a way that Annabel had helped her make her decision—and also glad they were still friends. In fact they were better friends now that the air was clear between them. She celebrated by going back to the counter and helping herself to a couple of Nonya cakes, the sweet, sticky coconut confections beloved of the west coast Chinese Malaysians. Her heart felt at peace at last, her decision to leave finally made for her.

'What the hell is this I hear?' Her peace was suddenly shattered as Andrew slid into the opposite seat, his face thunderous. 'Annabel said you were leaving the Ambassador!'

She breathed in deeply, needing the strength to face him with adequate control. 'Only when I have fulfilled my contract.'

There was a great earnestness in his eyes. 'Don't be ridiculous, Emily. You're at the beginning of a great career here.'

Courageously she resisted his onslaught. 'Forgive me for disagreeing with you, but I'm in the middle of a six-month contract here.'

'That's piffle. I won't hear of it.'

'Don't shout—everyone can hear you. And you have

nothing to do with it. I am over twenty-one and I make my own decisions.'

His eyes pleaded, and she tried to look away. 'Emily, Emily, you know you're only saying it. Someone has annoyed you — it must have been Sue Brown! I'll speak to that woman. I'll — never see her again. Emily, what am I going to do without you?'

Her heart ached, but she was determined. 'Exactly the same as you did before I came.'

'I cannot believe I'm hearing this!'

Emily looked across at him and felt her resolve crumbling. She knew that for the rest of her life she would always see this handsome face, the wild brown hair, sky-blue eyes and the lean jaw — and those gentle lips that looked so stern at times, yet could coax such pleasures from hers. . . She said gently, though her heart was breaking, 'There are times when one has to decide one way or the other. I've just decided that Singapore and I don't get on.'

'Does Gerald know?'

'I'm going to speak with him tonight.'

'He might ask you to marry him.' Was he really clutching at straws?

'You and I both know that it wouldn't work.'

Andrew sat back, and for the first time relaxed a little. 'So that's settled, then. One of my rivals out of the way.'

Was there no way of getting him off her back? 'It isn't a case of rivalry. It never was. Gerald and I made a mistake, and were sensible enough not to do anything hasty, that's all. Anyway, I should be discussing this with him, not with a total outsider like you.'

'Me? Outsider? Take care what you say, young lady. You and I have come a long way since the day we saved old Mahmoud's life at the Tanglin Palace.'

That was underhand, bringing up memories. 'That may be your assessment, Andrew, but you didn't consult me over it, I notice.'

He leaned over and took her hand, heedless of sideways glances from nurses at other tables. 'Then tell me, Emily. Do I really mean so little to you that you can just walk out of my country and out of my life?'

'I—consider us friends. In fact, I believe you are my only friend, though Annabel is a good sort, and so is Mai Li. But yes, I can and I will walk out of your life when my contract expires.' She smiled sadly. 'Even though I'll hate myself for it—just for a few days, I expect.'

'A few days. Woman, you don't get rid of me like that!'

'Andrew, I'm due back on duty. Please get out of my way.'

'But I haven't finished ranting at you yet.'

'Tough!' She handed him the cake plate. 'Have a Nonya cake. It might sweeten you for the afternoon clinic.' And she made her way out of the dining-room. When she looked back he was eating the other cake with a mournful expression on his face, and a lock of hair falling over his eyes. She loved him very much at that moment. But out of his life was the safest place to be. The ultimate loner—the eternal heartbreaker. Yes, she had made the right decision.

When she got back she expected Sue to have heard that she sat with Andrew at the dining table. But Sue was pleasant—she mustn't have heard the news yet. Emily started to go round with the medicines, only to hear Sue say in quite a normal voice, 'Old Mrs Alfonso was wondering when you were going to see her. There's another patient to be taken to the Haw Sing Centre— would you like to combine the two chores?'

'Sure, why not?' Her heart gave a little lurch, at the idea of seeing that place of Andrew's commitment.

'It's Mr Jahan. He's got no family, and doesn't want to go far from the Ambassador, so he asked to be transferred there. He can pay something towards his keep as well. The chief will be pleased.'

'Chief?' Did Sue not know who owned the Haw Sing? 'Which chief is that?'

'Whoever it is that runs that place.'

'You mean you've never even been over to see how it's run?'

'I believe them when they tell me it's a home from home. That's good enough for me.'

'You don't even know the chief's name?'

'No — do you?' She didn't wait for an answer. 'When I telephone, I always speak to the executive secretary. She's very sensible.'

'Oh.' Emily absorbed this news. Sue had known Andrew for so many months, and he had never confided in her what he did in his spare time. No wonder she was jealous — she probably thought he spent all his time with other women. 'Is Mr Jahan ready?'

'Yes. Get the doorman to call you an ambulance.'

'What time do you need me back?'

'There's no need to come back. You're off this afternoon. I'll see you tomorrow morning.'

'Right, Sister.' Emily longed to tell Sue she wasn't staying on at the Ambassador, but she decided to save up the news for a more appropriate time, when the message might make more impact. 'See you tomorrow.' And she went to take the wheelchair. 'So, Mr Jahan, you are leaving us.'

'Yes, but I do hope we'll see you in the home.'

'Well, now that I've started visiting, who knows?'

As they drove from the clinic block to the Haw Sing

Centre, Emily thought again about 'the chief'. In her eyes, Andrew Dashwood was one great guy. He had had an unfortunate experience in his early days — a married woman, it appeared — and had taken the totally selfless course of devoting himself to the poor and unlucky. Given his looks and charisma, there must have been a hundred women who thought they could tempt him from his lonely life — and all failed. Emily wasn't even going to try.

In the Haw Sing Centre, she looked for the executive secretary. Yes, the pleasant middle-aged lady who had received them last time. 'My name is Eleanor,' she said. 'I have been with Dr Dashwood since he founded the centre. In fact, my aunt helped him at the beginning — she was influential in the finance department.'

'I'm filled with admiration. Do you draw a salary?'

'Oh, no. Only expenses.'

'You spend all day and every day here — for love?'

'You could say that. And personal interest and spiritual enrichment, I suppose. Dr Dashwood is a very inspiring man.'

After Emily had chatted with Mrs Alfonso, and made sure Mr Jahan was settled in and taking tea with the man in the next flatlet, she went back to see Eleanor again. 'And are you quite content here?'

Eleanor's laugh pealed out. This was no recluse. 'Emily, I come from an extremely wealthy home. If I wanted, I could have a house in London, in the Bahamas, in Switzerland. But if I did I wouldn't have this chance of sharing in the hopes, fears and triumphs of my friends here. I tell you, I have travelled — and come home.'

During their chat, Emily asked if Eleanor had heard of the way the SEAH were trying to take over the Haw

Sing. 'I know about it because I'm an acquaintance of Gerald Montague. He's one of the co-directors.'

The down-to-earth Eleanor laughed again, a laugh that brightened the room around her. 'Oh, my dear, I don't mix with people like that!'

'No, I'm beginning to see why.' Eleanor was too wise to allow money to rule her life. Emily's admiration grew.

Eleanor went on, 'But yes, I have heard of the threat, and I am praying that Andrew doesn't give way under the pressure.'

'I can't believe that there is no other suitable site in the whole of the city of Singapore.'

'I can.' Eleanor nodded sadly, 'It's one of the hardest places in the world to buy land.'

Emily said, 'I did ask why he couldn't re-site the centre out in the suburbs, but Andrew insists that his residents would be lost away from the city.'

'That is very true, Emily.' And as Emily turned to go Eleanor held out her hand. 'It's been such a pleasure to meet you. My little nephew was one of your patients, and he never stops singing your praises and hoping you will come and see him soon.'

'Nephew? You can't mean — Kim?'

'Yes, his name is Kim. My aunt — his grandmother — is planning a grand dinner to thank you.'

'Eleanor, please tell your aunt that I'm — no good at grand dinners. Kim's recovery is a hundred times more than enough thanks.'

Later, Emily went to the Orchard Coffee House in Orchard Road, and treated herself to a seafood omelette and garlic salad. She didn't take a cab home. The city outside was too alluring. Instead she walked the length of Orchard Road, which took her a couple of hours, as she stopped and stared at everything, and spent time investigating the luxury shopping malls and precincts. Her eyes were dazzled by oriental silks, designer gowns, glittering gems, carvings of elaborate beauty and paintings so lavish that she wanted them all.

But as she turned off the main street towards Edinburgh Place, with aching feet and tired eyes, she thought again of the kind man, 'the chief', who lived among these luxuries, and yet chose to spend his own money on other people. Again his kindness dimmed her eyes with tears. She would go home and make a life for herself in London — but she would never meet a man of such consistent goodness. Or maybe she would meet a good man — but he would never look as devastating as Andrew, and his kisses would be pale and meaningless.

She let herself in, ready to drop from exhaustion. It was late, and the crickets were in good form tonight, shrilling their welcome among the grasses. When she heard the door being pushed open, she realised she hadn't locked it. Andrew said, 'You should be careful — there are a lot of shady people around this neck of the woods.'

She smiled, not getting out of the chair. 'Come in, Andrew.'

'What's this — you really are pleased to see me?'

'Yes.'

'Darling?' He positioned himself in front of her chair, lean legs akimbo, and in seconds she was in his arms. He held her close for a long time. She clung to him, wanting him badly, but not daring to show it by kissing him. He said against her ear, 'Darling Emily, you're upset.'

'A little. I suppose it's called growing up. Though at my age——'

He didn't mouth platitudes about her not being old.

'Growing is something that never stops, love. Not if you are wise and sweet and caring — as you are.'

She moved away from his embrace, though it was hard to let him go. 'Help yourself to coffee, Andrew.'

'OK. Want some?'

'All right.'

They sat together on the sofa, the coffee-mugs on the table before them. He said, 'I know you've been to Haw Sing again.'

'Yes.' She breathed in deeply, and went on, 'And I suppose you're expecting me to tell you how marvellous you are.'

'No.'

'That's good, because you're only living your life as you see fit, just like the rest of us.'

'How very sensible you are.'

'I liked Eleanor, though.'

'She liked you.' He paused. 'When you think about it, Emily, you've got a lot of friends in Singapore. How many did you say you had in London?'

She laughed, his remark breaking the tension of the sexual attraction between them. 'I didn't! It's my business.'

'There couldn't be anyone special if you gave up everything to follow Gerald.'

His arguments were becoming just a little bit too sensible and persuasive, so she teased him, daring to gaze into those remarkable eyes. 'Oh, Andrew, how do you know it wasn't a ploy? I might be using you just to make someone else jealous!'

'I don't mind, Emily. I don't mind if you use me or not — just as long as I can be with you a lot.' The sincerity in his eyes made her turn away.

She put her elbows on her knees, and gazed ahead.

'I give up. You have an answer to everything. I can't shock you, or surprise you.'

'You could surprise me by kissing me.'

She looked sideways at him, her elbows still on her knees, and her glance wary. 'No, that's what you expect me to do. I'm not going to kiss you ever again. I mean it, Andrew. You're a good friend, and I hope we meet some time in the future, but just now there's nothing to be gained by——'

She was in his arms then, so swiftly that she caught her breath as she looked up into his face, so close, so warm and so desirable. 'Shut up, my darling. Life is slipping past. Are you going to waste the best moments of it by talking?'

She said, without much conviction, 'That was the idea.'

'OK, so you want to debate your idea?'

He waited, and she gave up gracefully. 'No.'

She wasn't sure when the gentle early kisses became strong and insistent—so insistent that she lost all sight of her pricks of conscience with this man. Destiny took over, and somewhere inside her turbulent mind and melting body she realised that perhaps she wasn't meant to save herself for Mr Right. Maybe she was meant to lose her heart to this marvellous man, who would never be faithful, but who would give her the memories that she would recall in the September of her years. Roses in winter. . . It was so easy, now she had given in. They were made for each other, physically aware by instinct of what would give pleasure to the other.

Her clothes lay scattered on the floor, her hair against the cushions. He stood up to unbutton his trousers and she watched him through half-closed eyes as he threw his shirt down and gently lowered himself on to her, and took her close against his trembling heart. He's afraid, she thought. He's nervous — not sure if we ought to. 'Andrew,' she whispered, 'it's all right. I do know what I'm doing.'

'No. I don't think you do. My angelic Emily, I've been very selfish.' He bent his head between her breasts for a moment, and clung to her. 'Have I? I can't help it when you speak to me so softly.'

It was very hard to think clearly now, with warm skin against warm skin, every inch of his body hard and close and so very right against her yielding softness. Emily had not realised how lost and alone she felt, after being railed at by Sue Brown, and told by Annabel in no uncertain terms that she wasn't necessary in Gerald's life. Fortune, Kismet, Destiny, call it by any other name, had sent Andrew to her at this time of lowest ebb, and, although she could never call him her own, she could hold him in her arms and for a little while make them both happy in the wild joy of physical gratification.

She had never known such ecstatic abandon, such sweet fulfilment of her hidden and private desires. It had been right to wait until she met Andrew Dashwood. He had captured her soul with his goodness and thoughtfulness, and her body by the magnetic perfection of his young, strong body and limbs, his sweet and handsome face, never so beloved as now, when he lay beside her, his eyes closed with satiated passion, and his arms clasped around her with whispered words of honey after the volcanic explosion of their union.

He had covered her with a thin coverlet, and bent and whispered, 'Goodnight, my darling,' some time in the middle of the night.

Emily couldn't open her eyes for fear of losing the magic that still filled her satisfied body. But she murmured, as she heard him pulling on his clothes, 'I'm still going back home, Andrew. I have made up my mind.'

She felt his lips on her brow, grazing there for a moment and then brushing her cheek and her lips. He murmured, 'I think perhaps you're right, darling. But we'll always be best friends, won't we?'

'That goes without saying.' She ached to tell him how much she loved him, but that would spoil it. It would make her into one of the string of lovers who had tried to make Andrew Dashwood settle down to be a one-girl guy. No, she would keep him guessing about her feelings. He must know how deeply she cared for him, but she would never give him the satisfaction of hearing the words of love, nor the pain of having to decline when she pleaded with him to abandon his lonely bachelor life.

'I'll miss you. It will be like living in an echoing, empty house when you leave Singapore.'

His words sent a shiver of pure delight along her spine. She whispered, 'You say the nicest things, my dear. I suppose finding the right words comes with practice.'

She heard his intake of breath. Then a coolness in his sweet velvet voice. 'I've never in my life said that to anyone.'

'Even in Bangkok?'

'Oh, Emily, Emily, how could you?'

She rolled over then, covering herself modestly with the sheet, and opened her eyes. He was sitting on his heels at her side, one hand still lovingly stroking the curves of her body. She pushed back a strand of hair from her eyes, and said simply, 'I thought we were friends, Andrew. Good friends are frank with one another. I don't blame you for having girlfriends. It's only natural for a good-looking guy. Just don't pretend I'm the only one.'

He smiled, took her face in both his hands, and kissed her mouth slowly, lingeringly. Tendrils inside the satisfied Emily started uncurling, yearning, wanting him again. He murmured between kisses, 'I can see that my fine words cut no ice with you. Perhaps deeds might be more eloquent, then?' And with a sweep he pulled the coverlet from her naked body, and began to undo the buttons of his shirt. . .

CHAPTER ELEVEN

GERALD was sitting on his satin sofa, drinking champagne, and looking up at Emily. 'Say that again, Emily. Can I believe my ears? Just when you were getting used to my friends and my life, you honestly want to cry off? Call it a day, just like that?'

She nodded. 'I've had a very long think about it. I knew when I first came that I didn't fit in — but I believed that time would fix all that. It hasn't worked, has it, Gerald? I'm not happy in an environment that wants to turn old people out, send them to live somewhere else, just for the sake of your firm making more money.'

'Emmiekins, it isn't like that. They could be rehoused in even more luxury on the money that we're offering.'

'You just don't get it, do you? You think you and your cronies have the right to the best part of the city. Why are you denying these people their rights to live where they choose?'

'It's just the way things are, sweetie. You can't change human nature.'

'You don't have to sink to its worst depths, though.'

Gerald poured himself another glass of champagne. He didn't offer one to Emily. His voice was coldly sarcastic, as he said, 'I can see your Dr Dashwood has had quite a profound effect on you.'

Emily didn't reply at once. The mention of Andrew's name brought back the pulsating glory of the night he'd spent with her, the thrilling merging of two bodies so well attuned to each other that they knew without being taught just how to give each other the greatest pleasure, and to extend that pleasure throughout the warm tropical night. Gerald looked up curiously, waiting for an answer, and Emily said with as much dignity as she could muster, 'Your Dr Dashwood at least has a heart as well as money.'

'And he seems to have captured yours as well, sweetie.'

'I'm not one of his conquests, Gerald.'

'No, I can see that,' replied Gerald, cruelly adding, 'If you'd managed to snare him, you wouldn't be running off back to England.'

Emily turned to leave. 'There's no more to be said, Gerald. I suppose I've failed you, but I believe you thought you could mould me into your ideal woman just because you liked my looks. I'm sorry you're disappointed in me, but very glad we found out before we did anything foolish. Annabel is ideal for you.'

'Annabel? But she's a chum, not a woman.'

'That's not what I see from her angle. Think about it.'

Gerald stood up then. He seemed to have a sudden attack of decency. 'I say, I'm sorry I—said what I did about Dashwood. I didn't mean to hurt you. I mean— you've probably saved Annie's sight by getting her seen to so quickly. I suppose it's just my pride that's taken a thrashing. But I'll get over that, I dare say.'

'Good. I'm glad.'

Then the other side of him crept back maliciously, thrust where it hurt. 'And Emily—you and Dashwood have lost over the Haw Sing case. I'm going ahead with my plan to get that building.'

'You're going ahead with blackmailing Andrew! Then I really don't want to speak to you ever again.'

He leaned back and crossed one leg over the other.

With a smirk he said, 'Too bad, sweetie. That's showbusiness.'

'That's crooked business!' Emily hated him at that moment. 'I'll—I'll help Andrew fight you, Gerald, I promise. If you use that information about his past to get your way, I'll expose you as a blackmailer.'

'It's a doddle, Emily. He's too much of a pukka sahib to allow us to reveal the lady's name. He'll protect her, like the chivalrous fool he is.'

Emily looked at her former fiancé with something like loathing. 'To think I once thought you a decent man.' She went to the door. 'I'll fight you, Gerald. Until the SEAH name goes up over that building, I'll try and stop you.'

'What can you do? A simple little British nurse?'

'You forget I've met all your colleagues on the board. I know the people to speak to. I know you're a powerful man in Singapore, but I haven't yet lost my faith in human nature.'

'You're fighting for that old folks' home because you fancy its owner, I can see it. Well, you're wasting your time, Emily—you won't get him that way. He never sticks to one woman.'

'I know that, and I assure you I don't intend to chase after him. I work with him, and that's all. Who was it in Bangkok he had an affair with?'

'I don't know.' Gerald suddenly realised he had been trapped into giving the information. Emily had cleverly slipped the question in while speaking of something else, and it had tricked him into the admission. He tried to bluster. 'I don't have the name yet, but I've been promised it.'

'If you come up with enough money?' She left the room, saying angrily, 'How I despise you. I will always despise you.'

'Just don't get under my feet, you insignificant little woman. Don't interfere with my business, or something might just get out about *you*!'

She walked back to the clinic, feeling dirty after hearing so much unpleasantness. He was threatening her just to make her scared. How could she ever have admired this man? Only because he had hidden the nature of his business methods from her. Now that she knew, she couldn't bear to have anything more to do with him. What a lucky escape she had. If there hadn't been this wrangle over the Haw Sing Centre, she might never have seen the rotten underbelly of his success. She sighed as she pushed open the door of the ward. She knew she had very little chance of doing anything to dent Gerald's reputation in this city. He was right in one respect — she was an insignificant little woman, dabbling in things far too big and ugly for her.

She caught sight of Andrew chatting to Dr Mehtani, and again she felt the thrill of warmth to her loins that reminded her of her secret lover. But she wanted to speak to him on much more important business, and she made her way towards them, hoping for a quiet word.

She had reckoned without Sister Brown. 'Where exactly are you going, Nurse? The new admissions are at that end of the corridor.'

'Yes, Sister.' But she threw an agonised look towards Andrew, hoping he would notice it in the middle of his technical conversation. He didn't budge, and she knew she must wait until Sister Brown went off duty.

After taking the details and checking the pulses and blood-pressures and temperatures of the three admissions for operation, she went into Annabel's room. She was unhappy about Annabel now, wondering just how much of Gerald's devious business practices had rubbed off on to her. Annabel was such a devoted secretary, and she had adored Gerald for a long time. It was unlikely that she would wish to hear any bad about him.

'You're looking well.' In fact, fitted with a new brown wig, Annabel looked more natural, better than at any time before. Her face was thinner and gentler, and her eyes were bright, now that the offending growth had been removed from behind them. Emily said, smiling, 'You'll be home in a couple of days.'

Annabel looked earnestly at her. 'You've been to see him?'

'Yes,' she replied simply. 'I told him I'd made up my mind to go home. He agreed—he said it was only his pride that was hurt, and he'd soon get over that.'

'And—did he mention me?'

'Only to say how well you were looking. And no—I didn't even mention that I'd talked to you about this first.'

'Thank you. Thank you very much, Emily.' Annabel's eyes were very sincere, and Emily bent and kissed her cheek.

She said, 'I have to ask you this. How much do you know about his—business methods?'

'Oh, he works very near the knuckle—but then, my dear, all these really big people do.'

Emily stared at her. 'You don't mind it?'

'I accept it. Dog eat dog, you see.'

'I don't mind dog eating dog. It's when he consumes a tiny defenceless rabbit that it hurts.'

Annabel saw through her, and nodded. 'You're talking about Haw Sing, aren't you? I do see your point of view, Emily, but it's naïve in this day and age to expect little people to win in matters like this. But out of thanks for what you did for me I'll stay out of this one—let things happen without helping in any way. Is that a deal?'

Emily nodded. It was all she could hope for. 'I appreciate it.'

It was when Emily was sent up to Theatre to bring some notes and X-rays down that Andrew suddenly waylaid her in Recovery's side-room. 'What's the matter, love? You looked worried.'

She looked about her, afraid that Sue Brown would pop up out of the linen cupboard. She said, 'I'll tell you more later when there's more time, but I thought you should know that Gerald doesn't have the name of your—indiscretion—in Thailand. His informant is waiting for more money before he'll tell.'

'Typical. What a louse!' But Andrew looked relieved. 'Thanks a million, Emily—I think I might just be able to find out who the louse is in time to stop him.' He bent and kissed her cheek, and she drew in a sudden breath at the warmth of his lips and the electricity from him that seemed to burn an impression in her skin. Then he walked out of the room swiftly before anyone caught them together.

There was a commotion in the corridor as she returned to the ward, and Emily stood back as a stretcher was wheeled in. Sister Brown was coping with her usual efficiency. 'An accident in Orchard Road. Young man—unconscious. The ambulance staff have checked his airway, and we must just wait for the doctors. Stay with him, would you, Nurse?'

'Yes, of course.' Emily watched as the patient was splinted on to a bed. He appeared in a deep coma, but there were no marks of trauma on his body. 'Do you know where he was hit?'

'There's no history. He was just found on the pavement.'

Emily sat at the bedside, monitoring his pulse from time to time. It was Mai Li who stopped on her way to the ward, and said, 'Probably a gangland problem. It's usually the Triads when someone young and male is brought in like this.'

'Gangland!' Emily looked wary. 'Shouldn't he be taken to the General Hospital? We're totally private.'

'They're full. Oh, here's the doctor. I'll see you later, Emily, and you can tell me if I'm right.'

Andrew came in with his familiar long strides, and Emily couldn't hold back a little smile of relief and gladness just to see him. He exchanged a brief look with her, a fleeting look but one in which she felt the waves of affection between them almost tangibly. But then he was feeling the patient's pulse, and opening the eyes to see the pupils and inside the eyes with his torch. He examined the reflex in the jaw, and carefully felt the neck. While his practised fingers were moving from biceps and triceps reflex tests to the supinator response, he said to Emily, 'What's happened to Sue? How come she's allowing you to stay here with me?'

'I've no idea. It was Sue who told me to sit with him. I say, is it drugs? I saw he had very tiny pupils, and his supinator response is very diminished.'

'I think almost definitely.' Andrew had moved to the knee jerk, which was very weak, and the ankle, where the response to the sharp tap on the Achilles' tendon was also very slack. Finally he drew the tip of his tendon hammer up from heel to toe on the sole of each foot. On the left there was no response at all, while on the right the toes jerked very slightly upwards. 'Mmm — dorsiflexion. Yes, better intubate, Emily. He'll need some help with his breathing.'

'Mai Li said it might be gangland?' Emily's eyes were wide.

Andrew smiled at her. 'The cause doesn't matter to us — we're just here to pick up the pieces. But yes — the Triads have some nasty little habits. They can overdose the victim with morphine, like this fellow. But they can also induce coma by hitting the neck in such a way as to leave no mark on the body but the blow damages the brain-stem.'

'Wow!'

He said gently, 'Your sheltered life has been opened up a bit since coming to Singapore?'

'It certainly has.'

He put his tendon hammer in the pocket of his white coat and went to her. 'In nice ways as well as bad?' He put his hands on her shoulders.

She nodded, looking up at him, trying not to show her besottedness in her eyes. Her voice was as impersonal as she could manage. 'In very nice ways. I'll just get a tube.'

'Don't walk out on me. You'll be leaving in a few short months, and I won't have seen enough of you, darling. I was going to ask you to stay on.'

'Again? We've been over that.'

'Maybe we could go over it again over dinner?'

There was nothing she wanted more, but she prevaricated. 'You aren't going to Haw Sing?'

'Yes. Want to come along?'

'Yes, please. I'd like to talk to Eleanor.'

'Right, then we'll go together. I'll call for you at six.'

'I only come off at six.'

'I'll call for you at five past!' And he went out of the room, leaving Emily to intubate the patient in case his breathing reflexes were too weak to keep him adequately oxygenated. She brought an oxygen cylinder. It might be needed.

While she waited to see if he would come round, she

pondered on the conversation she had just had with Andrew. He had sounded so loving, so caring. He quite clearly wanted to be with her tonight. Yet she knew she mustn't depend on his faithfulness. A free spirit. He hated the thought of being tied down. It was hard to do, but she knew that if she wanted his friendship she must accept him for what he was, and expect nothing from him but the pleasure of his company when he chose to bestow it.

Sue Brown came in. 'No change? Then we'd better get him into Intensive Care. I can't spare a nurse to sit with him full time.' Her manner was businesslike, but not curt or unfriendly. She must have known that Emily and Andrew had been together with the patient, yet she was displaying no signs of the usual jealousy or irritation.

Emily decided now was a good time to tell Sue about her plans. She said, 'Sister, I won't be renewing my contract when my six months is up.'

Sue looked surprised. 'No? I thought you enjoyed the work here. You've had some spectacular successes with individual patients.'

'I do like the work—and the patients.'

'Then why not give us another year? I can get a contract drawn up that would suit your hours, you know.'

Totally surprised at Sue's sudden change of attitude, Emily bit back her questions, and just said, 'I think perhaps I don't fit in in Singapore. It's been an interesting episode, but life here is very different. I don't think I belong here.'

'Well, I hope I can change your mind before your time is up.' And Sue bustled off, leaving Emily very mystified.

Promptly at six-five Andrew tapped on her door. As

soon as he was in the room he took her in his arms, hugging her to him as though she was someone very precious. 'I wanted to do that all day.'

She nestled against him for a moment, but said, 'You mustn't stay tonight.'

He drew back so that he could look into her eyes, and said in his tenderest voice, 'Shall we see what we feel like later on? Business before pleasure.'

'I won't change my mind, Andrew.'

'We won't argue.'

'You think you can persuade me, don't you? Well, that shows a very cocky sort of nature.'

'I am what I am, love. Are you ready?'

'Yes.' They walked together across the grass, Andrew's arm gently resting on her shoulder. She said, 'Have you done anything about the louse from Bangkok?'

'I've made some enquiries.'

'Gerald says you're too much of a gentleman to take chances. He says you'll give in to save the lady's reputation.'

He sighed. 'He's right, of course. If it were only my own reputation, I'd take a chance and tell him to publish and be damned. But it isn't fair on — on her.'

'So because of that you're going to sell Haw Sing?' It didn't seem right to give in so easily.

'I might. But all is not lost yet.'

'If you find the louse?'

'*When* I find the louse!'

'I'm glad, Andrew. I'm glad you're fighting him.'

'It's beginning to mean something to you.'

'Yes. Somehow in this bustling place, with so many people "on the make" at any price, Haw Sing is a place where people matter. It's become a bit of a symbol to me. I'd just hate to see it go. I mean to fight for it.'

Andrew stopped walking. They were standing in the street, almost at the entrance to the Haw Sing building. Passers-by milled past them as they stood, oblivious of anything but each other, and he said, 'Apart from Eleanor, Emily, darling, you're the only other person who has ever stood by me — ever said anything as supportive as that about this place.'

'I mean it. If there's anything I can do, please tell me.'

'Find me a physiotherapist. We desperately need one, part-time.'

'OK, I'll ask around.'

'Oh, Emily, you are an angel — an angel sent from heaven to give me hope again!'

'Don't talk like a Victorian novel, love.'

He bent and kissed her forehead, then, clutching her close to him, ran up the steps into the building. Emily was pleased to see Eleanor's face light up as they came into the archway through to the lounge. 'You run in here like a couple of mischievous children,' she laughed. 'I was just on the point of sending you packing!'

Andrew gave her a little hug. 'Now, I'll just go and check on the old lady. Back in a moment. Emily, wander wherever you like. See you in a minute.'

Eleanor looked after the whirlwind and smiled again. 'Oh, Emily, I've never seen him so happy. You've been so good for him.'

Emily felt a little guilty at this. 'But I've done nothing. I'm just full of empty promises and hopes. I've done nothing to help him at all.'

'Perhaps you help him just by being at his side?'

'Oh, no — how can you say so?'

'I do believe my own eyes.' Eleanor's look was sympathetic. She was too clever not to know exactly what was happening—she had known Andrew a long time.

When Andrew came back, Emily had been doing her own rounds of the home, and chatting to the residents. The more she saw of them, the more strongly she felt how cynical it was to expect them to be moved out as though they were articles of second-hand furniture instead of delightful human beings. Oh, please, please, let Andrew find that informer before Gerald bribes him! she thought. But she kept her prayers quiet, knowing so well just how near they were to losing out to Gerald and his SEAH.

Eleanor said as they were leaving, 'I have an invitation for you from my aunt.'

'The rich old lady?'

'Yes, Kim's grandmother. She would like you both to go to dinner next Saturday. She has also invited the Wangs. Lennie is staying with Kim for a few days during the holidays. It will be a happy party.'

'It will if you'll be there.' Andrew showed his appreciation of the ever-cheerful Eleanor. 'I'll be pleased to accept. How about you, Emily?'

'I think I'm free, Eleanor, but my ward sister sometimes gives me unexpected duties.'

'Then that's settled. How nice. I look forward to it very much. Aunt will send the Rolls for you.'

Excited about seeing the boys, Emily forgot to be impressed by the talk of a Rolls-Royce. 'What can I bring for the boys?'

'Just yourself, Emily. They are very fond of you.'

As they walked down the steps to the street, Andrew murmured, 'Another family of fans! How many friends did you say you had in London?'

She laughed. 'At it again, Dashwood? You won't change my mind, you know.'

They ate simply at a small, secluded basement restaurant, dining on succulent prawns and *or luah* — an oyster omelette with fresh vegetables and delicate saffron rice. Their conversation never faltered, as at first they joked with each other, and then later chatted about the Haw Sing, and how many hours a week they needed a physiotherapist to keep the stiffer patients mobile. 'I don't mind running a dancing class, Andrew. But I don't know how well it would go down here. In the Lester I took a group for ballroom dancing, and it improved their balance and their general fitness remarkably. It made them happier too — a lot of them were lonely, and in ballroom dancing you just have to reach out and hold someone else.'

He looked soulfully across the table, his piercing blue eyes powerfully beautiful and expressive. 'You know, Emily, that sounds like a perfect motto for you and me.'

'Motto?'

He repeated her words. 'You just have to reach out and hold someone else.' His voice was husky and expressive.

She swallowed the lump in her throat, and made light of his remark. 'Yes, my lad, and you make a habit of it!'

He protested, gently, 'I'm not as bad as you think. I date girls, yes, but I never want anyone to fall for me.'

'Then you'd better stop dating them, and fast!'

'Sue is the only one who has shown any hurt. I'm truly sorry about that, but I never encouraged her. She had a boyfriend, and instead of hanging on to him she ditched him for me after I'd taken her out for dinner just once. I was appalled. But she's clung on rather pathetically. I like her very much. She was a fun person before she got this obsession. I wish she'd be my friend again.'

Emily watched him. Yes, there was affection there. Sue had frightened him off, that was certain, but he still liked her a lot. When Emily went home to England, Sue would probably benefit the most. Emily said gently, 'I do hope you'll be happy—really happy, one day. I know your life is very fulfilled and satisfactory. But there's something rather sad about a bachelor.'

He nodded at her wisdom with a suitably grave face. 'And what about a spinster?'

Emily sat up and smiled. 'She is just sensible enough not to get caught and turned into a skivvy. There's something admirable about a spinster.'

He leaned back in his chair and returned the smile. 'So you're a secret feminist, Emily?'

'Oh, there's no secret about it.'

'I'm glad you're a feminist, because I am, too. That's why I don't believe in expecting women to be at my beck and call. And why I sew on my own buttons— well, I get the dry-cleaners to do my repairs, but it's the principle that counts.'

'You're quite hopeless!' Emily couldn't help laughing again. She leaned closer across the table and said softly, 'Hopeless, but very nice.'

They walked back. It was as though they wanted to prolong the evening. For it never to end. So they sauntered through the parks, and down to the waterfront past the cathedral and the cricket club. The harbour was alive with twinkling lights, and the Merlion, the great statue looking out over the Singapore river, spurted a floodlit stream of water out in a sparkling rainbow in the darkness. He said, 'You're acclimatised now. You haven't complained of the heat.'

'It's wonderful. Just right.'

'I'm glad.' He drew her close and kissed her. Then they took a cab back to the Bungalow Hari Raya. Emily paused at the door. Andrew said, 'Goodnight, my dearest. Thank you for one of the loveliest days of my life.'

'But—I did nothing.'

'Go on doing it like that and I'll be a happy man.' They looked into one another's eyes, and she hoped he couldn't read the surging love in her face, the rush of affection that threatened to make her cry with the pain of it. He said gently, with a little shake of his head, 'I'm going to miss you so very much when you go.' Then he touched her cheek, turned on his heel, and walked off into the darkness.

CHAPTER TWELVE

MADAME KIM poured delicate jasmine tea into tiny transparent cups after the meal. Her old hand shook, but no one dared to help her. She was the hostess, and the entire table deferred to her position and authority. A maid handed round the cups. Madame said, 'Kim, you and Lennie may go and play now. Take your tablets, then you may have an hour's relaxation before bedtime.'

'Yes, Grandmama. Thank you, Grandmama. A whole hour!' The boys had been bursting to go and play with their toys, but had waited with barely concealed impatience for permission. They said goodnight, very politely, and walked from the elegant mahogany and gold dining-room, with its crystal chandeliers making the entire room sparkle. But the moment they were out of the room, the sound of their eager running feet was clearly audible from the dining-room. There was a universal smile of indulgence. Madame said, 'I thought I might never hear that happy sound again. It is a great joy to me that the boys are well again.'

Mrs Wang said, 'It has been a hard time for us all. I also am very grateful that my son is returned to health, but the best thing is that they have found a friend. They are inseparable.'

Madame said, 'You are kind to leave him here for another few days.'

Mr Wang, a taciturn man with a battered face, echoed his wife's sentiments. 'We like Lennie to be so noisy—so normal. But if he is a nuisance, I'll come and fetch him at once.'

But Madame wouldn't hear of it. Sipping her tea, she said, 'We will bring him to the door, of course. And please do not think I allow them to stay up so late every night. It is only tonight, as a treat because their favourite nurse and doctor came to see them.'

Eleanor had shown Emily round the grand seaside villa in Pasir Ris, along the northern shore of the island. It was furnished in the old Chinese style with great taste, and was filled with exquisite jade and pearl ornaments and figurines. Now, as the Wangs took their leave, she suggested that they all—Madame and Eleanor, Andrew and Emily—adjourn to the balcony where they could look out over the Straits of Johore, and watch the fireflies flickering among the bushes, and the lights of the fishermen out in the straits. 'And perhaps Andrew would like a small brandy?'

'Thank you, but I shall be driving.'

'Then a little mineral water.' An inlaid tray with iced water was placed deferentially between them, with crystal bowls of tiny hand-made peppermints.

Emily said, 'What a perfect end to a lovely meal.'

'A dinner? Not enough reward, my dear, for all you did for my grandson.'

Emily assured her that it had been a wonderful experience.

'Then we must make sure you come again.'

Eleanor said, 'Did you know, Aunt, that Emily is not planning to stay in Singapore?'

Madame was surprised. 'Is the climate too much for you, my dear?'

'No, I like the heat now.'

'Then you cannot like the people?'

Emily laughed. 'Oh, I do, I do. I have some very good friends.'

'Then I cannot possibly see why you should go back to a cold country when your friends are here.'

Andrew interrupted, and in the darkness his voice was thrilling and intimate. 'I am hoping she will see for herself before she makes such a big mistake, Madame Kim. The Haw Sing, for example, needs her very badly. Did you know she starts teaching the residents ballroom dancing next week?'

Madame's eyes sparkled. The narrow dark eyes were suddenly alive with memories. 'Oh, Emily, how very nice. That takes me back to the old days — before the war. Oh, the dances we used to have in the old house...'

'Then you must know the dances better than I.'

'I suppose I might.' Madame looked girlish. 'Can you imagine me doing the Charleston?'

All her majesty and dignity faded, as she related long-ago stories of life among the rich in pre-war Singapore. The evening ended on this very happy note, with laughter ringing over the park towards the water. But as they were rising, Madame halted them with a little wave of her hand. 'Emily, you refused to take a gift from me.'

'Well, yes, I did — but I hope it wasn't rude of me.'

'Not rude at all. I hope you won't refuse this.' And the silent-footed maid entered with a jade box etched in gold filigree, intricately carved and beautifully designed. 'It belonged to my mother. Will you accept it, Emily? Perhaps it will do to hold your jewels when you are married.'

Emily was speechless for a moment. 'It's — such an honour,' she stammered.

'The honour will be mine if you accept.'

Emily suddenly bent and kissed the old lady's papery cheek. 'It's too beautiful for me, Madame Kim, but I'll accept it very gratefully, and try to live up to such a priceless thing.'

'I think it suits you very well.' She rose to see them to the door. 'There is one condition, Emily——'

'Yes, anything.'

'Don't open it until a week from today.'

'There's something in it. Oh, this is too much.'

'It is a trifle, but I think you will like it. Remember now, open it in one week's time.'

'How exciting. I do promise.'

'And I look forward to seeing you both again soon.'

On the journey back, Emily protested that it was all wrong that she should get such an expensive gift when Andrew received nothing. But he was unperturbed. 'I'm not a poor man. Why should she shower me with gold and jade?'

'It's like you, Andrew, not to care about possessions. That's not the way Gerald thinks. He is wealthy and he just wants to be even wealthier.'

Andrew put a hand briefly on her knee. 'Shall we forget that creep? And—please can I be with you when you open the box next week?'

'Oh, yes, I'd like that. It was a strange promise, but of course I'll wait until I'm allowed to open it. Where shall we have the grand opening?'

'My place,' he said shortly. 'You've never been to my place.'

She felt a shiver of premonition. 'You've never invited me.'

'I've never invited anyone.' The words hung in the air, a statement that didn't need an answer, but possibly did need an explanation. He didn't offer any explanation.

When they got back to Emily's flat, she didn't ask Andrew in. She held her head high, determined not to mind if he just went home. But she felt empty already—it was only a tiny hint of the enormous heartache she knew she would feel when she walked out of his life and on to that plane back to Heathrow.

'What was that little sigh about?' Andrew had been watching her.

'I didn't sigh.'

'Oh?' There was amusement in his eyes. They both knew she was wrong. Then the welcome words, 'I think I ought to see you safely inside tonight, Emily—considering the value of that little box. In fact, I ought to make sure we find a secure hiding place for it.'

'Thank you.' She allowed him in, glad that there was a genuine reason. 'Would you like coffee?'

'It's tempting, but let's find a home for your mystery gift first, darling.' He moved round the room, looking around. 'You haven't any really safe place here, have you?'

'No. Maybe I should strengthen the lock?'

'Would you like me to look after it for you?'

Emily hesitated. 'It's a kind thought, but I think Madame wanted me to have it because of its beauty—and I couldn't look at it if you kept it.'

'Then I have the answer. Leave it lying around, and surround it with other, cheaper ornaments. A thief would always assume that anything valuable would be locked away.'

Emily looked at him, so handsome and so desirable in his white dinner-jacket—every woman's dream of a perfect man. She began to smile. 'Oh, Andrew, what a devious mind you have!'

'I am what I am, my dear. You know me now.'

'I think so.'

She searched for some message in his eyes, but his face was blank. She couldn't read those eyes, which sometimes had been so loving and open. He said carefully, 'I know you are as free a spirit as I am, Emily.'

She looked at him and said, 'That's true.' But she felt she had to break the sudden stiffness between them. She added, 'And I don't like arguing with you, Andrew. If I've offended you, I apologise. There is enough hurt in the world without friends arguing.'

In the stillness they heard the melodious trill of a nightingale in the trees outside her window. Then suddenly they turned to each other as though worked by a single switch, and she clung to him, longing to tell him how much she had missed his kisses. But she dared not, so she said nothing, and after a while he released her. He said, practically, 'Never mind coffee. I'll see you around. And I'll come for you next week so that we can settle our curiosity over what's in the box together.'

She said, 'I was thinking about next week, Andrew. It's the board meeting at the Tanglin Palace — to decide what to do about you if you won't sell. They'll vote you off the board, Andrew.'

'I know. That doesn't hurt. But it's what they'll do to my Haw Sing friends that does.'

Emily watched his beloved face, and saw how sad his eyes could be. 'Let's hope you find that man Gerald's after. We could maybe get his name from Annabel. Without him there'll be no blackmail threat.'

'That's an idea, Emily. I'll try Annabel tomorrow.' He bent and kissed her very tenderly, very briefly, as though she might break.

* * *

Emily did a lot of sitting around and thinking for the next couple of days. She was being brutally honest with herself now. It wasn't Singapore she was running away from, but Andrew. She knew she wouldn't be able to live here, seeing him daily, yet knowing that he belonged to no one, and didn't want anything else in his life. If only I could be strong, and not let this 'being in love' thing bother me, she said to herself. It's never been like this before. No human being has consumed me like this. There'll never be another Andrew in my life. I'll end up taking over from Eleanor, a kindly maiden lady giving my life to others.

When she went to the Haw Sing to give her first dancing lesson with a small cassette player and some tapes begged and borrowed from nurses and friends at the hospital, Emily looked at Eleanor with new eyes. This is me, she thought. This is how I'll be. Spoilt for any other man by loving my ideal too much.

Eleanor was observant. 'You're thoughtful, Emily. What's bothering you? I thought the lesson went very well.'

'The residents loved it. I think the class will be larger next week, as some of them forget their shyness!'

'What is on your mind, my dear? You haven't opened your gift box yet?'

'Oh, no, I made a promise. Do you know what is in it?'

'I? Oh, no. Aunt isn't the kind of person to exchange confidences. But I will tell you that she is a very perceptive lady. All her gifts are very appropriate.'

'Oh, well—it will be a ticket home, then.'

'Emily, you are sad!'

'Forget me, Eleanor. Tell me about yourself. Why didn't such a lovely lady as you ever marry?'

Eleanor's famous laughter echoed round the little

lounge. 'Too much choice, dear! I told you—I travelled a lot, picking and choosing who to be friends with. I didn't want to tie myself down to one man—there were so many nice fellows in Europe and in San Francisco. . .' Her voice trailed away for a moment. 'I didn't meet the one who would have been just right. So I never settled down as a wife. I don't regret it. Now I'm past the age of prinking in the mirror and caring about my face, I find I have a great many friends of both sexes. I love my life, Emily. Is that hard to understand for a young thing like you?'

'Not hard at all.'

'You're such a sweet girl. I'll really hate it when you go, but I'll come and visit you on your lonely, cold little island and bring some Singapore sun!'

Emily was thinking over those four little words, as she sat beside the latest craniotomy patient, and soothed her pain as she changed her dressings and adjusted her drainage tubes, and assured her that all their wigs were the latest fashion. 'Lonely, cold little island. . .' Was that what she really wanted? Maybe she could be lonely here instead, on a lonely warm little island? But it would have to be on the far side of the island, far away from the Ambassador Clinic, where a certain tall, blue-eyed medic would not be constantly under her feet and in her thoughts.

The phone rang. 'Emily? Have you got a minute?'

'Sure.' Sue Brown didn't usually call her by her first name at work. But perhaps she had been out with Andrew again. Emily hadn't seen him to speak to for several days. She walked along to Sue's office—only to find Marilyn Boon in there with Sue. 'Hello, Marilyn,' she said. 'You're looking better at last. It's not been an easy few weeks with that rotten infection. I bet you never want to hear the word "Klebsiella" again!'

Marilyn was very cheerful. 'It gave me lots of time to think, and I decided that I want to travel before I retire. How is life in the Royal Lester Hospital?'

'Well, I enjoyed it—but I like my lonely, cold little island. You might not.'

'That's not how I see Britain. I'd like to do a study tour. But I need a replacement here, Emily, and, to cut a long story short, the management would like you to take over from me.'

'Me? Executive sister?' Emily felt as though someone had hit her. She looked at Sue. 'I'd be your boss!' she said with a smile.

'And I'd deserve anything you cared to throw at me, Emily. I've been very silly about you. You can't help being pretty. So when Marilyn asked my opinion, I agreed that you were the best woman for the job.'

Emily said, 'I was planning on going home. . .'

'You've bought your ticket?' asked Marilyn robustly.

'No.'

'Good. Then I'll give you three days to think it over.'

'It's tempting. . .' But not in the same hospital as Andrew. Oh, no, it would never work. 'Three days? I'll give you an answer as soon as I can. But it would mean a job for life, wouldn't it?'

'Yes. It's a commitment.'

Emily smiled at the two women. They'd paid her a great compliment, but her heart was broken at the moment, and that wasn't the best time to make a lifetime decision. 'I'll—just get back to work.'

After work, she chatted for a while to her replacement staff nurse. Tomorrow was the day to open the box, and she had watched it each day as though it were alive. She saw Andrew leaving by the side-door, not turning to wave or say goodbye, not even to Sue.

And then Sue was saying, 'How about coming for a drink, Emily? I've been a bit of a swine, and it isn't really me. I'd like to explain. See you at the main entrance when you've had a chance to change?'

'Thanks, I will.'

She didn't dress up—just a quick shower and a cotton dress, sandals and no jewellery. It was a good feeling to make it up with Sue, and she was prompt at the main door. 'Where are we going?'

'I thought you'd like to see a little place I used to drive past. I've never been inside, but I've always been curious.'

'Sounds highly mysterious.'

'Sure—but I bet the drinks are just fine.' Sue had a small Toyota, and the girls spent the journey through the fascinating streets of Little India, along the Serangoon Road, Buffalo Road and Lavender Street, discussing the merits of a Japanese car. There were quite grand houses mingled with blocks of ordinary little flats, and the smell of incense and coriander permeated the streets. Raven-haired women in saris of vivid colours, edged quite shamelessly in lovely borders of gold and silver, walked along with incongruous plastic carrier bags doing the weekly shopping.

'I love this place. What a fascinating area to live. And the restaurants! You'd never go hungry.'

'I thought you might like it. This is where we're going.' And Sue turned into a tiny cul-de-sac, where a little painted wooden bungalow stood amid a pocket handkerchief of a garden.

'But this is a private house.'

'It's all right. It belongs to a good friend of mine. We're expected.' And Sue locked the car door, and led the way to an open door with a tiny trellis covered with clematis. It was too dark inside to see anything, but Sue boldly knocked on the door, and called, 'Anyone home?'

Emily paused when a man's voice answered, 'Come on in.'

Sue said, 'Go on. It's quite safe. He's housetrained.' And Emily made out a tall figure coming to the door. He was barefoot, in oriental style, and he wore trousers and a batik shirt. It was Andrew Dashwood.

'Come in, Emily. Welcome to my home.'

She stood for a moment, unsure if she really was welcome, but he reached out and took her hand, and when he was close she read the hunger in his eyes. Feeling suddenly rather hot, she slipped off her sandals, and went in, turning to wait for Sue. But the Toyota engine was already running, and Andrew said, 'She's gone, Emily.'

'But why? Why the mystery?'

'She wanted to prove to you that there's nothing between us. She's gone back to her boyfriend.'

'Honestly?'

'Honestly.'

Emily looked around the tiny room. It was like a miniature house, with table, chairs and a sofa. There seemed to be a small kitchen behind, and a bathroom. 'Is this all you have?'

'What more do I need?'

'It's absolutely charming.'

'I think so. And the cooking is good.' He indicated a restaurant just round the corner. 'Can I offer you a drink?'

'Yes — please.'

Andrew went to the table, and there was suddenly a

very loud pop. Emily laughed. 'You and champagne! I don't believe it.'

'Well, it's a special occasion. To toast your new job.' He brought two foaming glasses, and, laughing, they clinked them and drank.

'It's nice of you, Andrew. And nice of Sue, too. But I'm not staying. I couldn't.'

He set down his glass and moved to sit beside her. 'Darling, please stay. It would break my heart to lose you.' His voice cracked, and he paused and cleared his throat. 'I've never in my life cared so much for anyone. I'm not a wealthy man, but you've seen the sort of life I lead. If you will, Emily, I'd be very honoured if you'd share it for the next hundred years or so. Will you? I've never proposed before, so I don't know if I'm doing it right?'

'Is there a wrong way?' she whispered, unsure what to say when her heart was singing like a choir of heavenly angels.

'Are you saying yes?'

Her voice was husky with emotion. 'Yes—I think I am. My mind is in such a whirl——' and Andrew proceded to increase her confusion by kissing her. It was meant to be one kiss, but their hunger for one another was too strong, and she kissed him wildly and passionately, surrendering herself as she had yearned to do but dared not before. He got up and quietly locked the door, turned on the fan, and laid her on his exotic oriental couch before gently undressing her and himself. But desire overcame his gentleness, and soon she felt the strength of him and the power and the glory of him as they became one in a crescendo of emotion. Time vanished. He took her to him twice, and still they locked together, neither willing to allow the other any rest. She strained against him, trying to undo all the frustrations of her unrequited days of loneliness, arched herself to him and took him to her.

'My darling, you're magnificent.' His voice broke with emotion as they lay, warm limbs entwined. He squeezed her against him. 'I feel very inhospitable. I invited you to dinner, and it's after midnight.' He kissed her body, all of it his, smoothed his cheek against her belly and she meshed her fingers in his tangled hair. 'I've nothing to eat. I only sleep here.'

'Then come back to Hari Raya and I'll make you bacon and eggs.'

'Sounds wonderful.' She hardly remembered what they talked of on the journey back to her flat, but it had a lot to do with mutual admiration and how fantastic the future was going to be. They walked across the garden together, along the winding path, arms firmly round the other and hearts still beating strongly in the forceful need to prove their love yet again.

Emily found some green salad, cheese and olives, while Andrew ground some coffee and filtered it. 'Is this supper or breakfast?'

'Breakfast!' Andrew suddenly pointed to the jade box. 'It's tomorrow, darling. You can open your present now. Shall I get it for you?'

'Have you any idea what it could be?'

'No, no idea. With her money, she's bound to have some fabulous jewels.' He carried the box to her, shaking it a little. 'Nothing rattles.'

She held out her hands and took it gingerly. The lid came off easily. 'It's a letter—some papers.' Emily took them out and straightened them.

Andrew said, his voice hushed, 'It looks like title deeds.'

'There's her letter here. My, what neat handwriting.

Listen, Andrew, oh, listen to this!' She read aloud, her voice shaking with emotion.

> My dear Emily, I find I am in a position to give you a gift you will really appreciate. It gives me great pleasure to give to you both an alternative site in central Singapore, which you can sell to your SEAH board for a very large sum. I have known for some time of the threat to the Haw Sing Centre, and I know Eleanor is as pleased as I am that now it will be left in peace to its residents and its dedicated staff. With the income from this property, the Haw Sing will no longer have financial worries. With my continued good wishes for your future happiness, Madame Kim Sie Kai.'

Andrew had risen to his feet as she read, and now he stood erect, his eyes shining. 'God bless that lady!'

Madame had indeed chosen the most appropriate gift of all. Emily sat, hugging herself with joy. 'Oh, Andrew, how I wish I were going to that meeting today. I can just see their faces when you show them these deeds. Is it near Haw Sing?'

'Only a few blocks away. A prime site — all shops and offices, so no one suffers by losing a home.'

She looked up at him with love in her eyes. 'I think I want to cry.'

He was beside her in a flash, his arms cradling her. 'Tell me, little Emily, are you going to stay in Singapore now?'

Her arms crept up behind his head, to pull him down to her. 'I might,' she whispered, her cheek against his.

He said between kisses, 'I didn't sleep with Sue, you know.'

'It doesn't matter.' But it did, and she was glad.

'I lost my heart and soul to you in that first second I

saw you in the Tanglin Palace. I felt some sort of explosion in my head when I saw that beautiful girl just sitting, looking at me. My ideal woman, there in the flesh! I told myself that if I couldn't get her, then no one else would do.'

'But I might have been a crook. How can you tell by appearances, Andrew?'

'Does love work by logic, darling?'

'No,' she whispered. The sun was coming up brightly now, and the lovers stood at the window, feeling the heat of its rays. 'No, thank goodness!'

'There's something tremendous in a dawning,' said Andrew. 'A new beginning, and a day of such immense promise.'

'A day — and a lifetime,' she said.

He kissed her cheek as they stood side by side, arms locked. 'A lifetime is a long time. I can't promise an easy ride, Emily. I've been a loner all my life.'

She turned to him, thrilling to the intensity of his eyes. 'I don't ask for an easy ride, darling. Only that you and I will face everything together.'

'Now that sounds like good common sense to me.' He turned her to face him. 'And a lot of fun. Maybe today we should start filling up that jewel box of yours by buying a Singapore diamond?'

There was only one reply to that, and it was a silent one, and it lasted a long time. . .

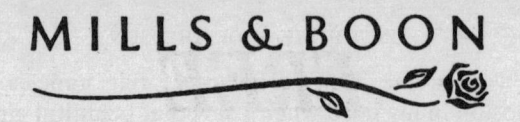

MILLS & BOON

LOVE ON CALL

The books for enjoyment this month are:

PICKING UP THE PIECES Caroline Anderson
IN THE HEAT OF THE SUN Jenny Ashe
LEGACY OF SHADOWS Marion Lennox
LONG HOT SUMMER Margaret O'Neill

♥ ♥ ♥ ♥ ♥

Treats in store!

Watch next month for the following absorbing stories:

NO MORE SECRETS Lilian Darcy
TILL SUMMER ENDS Hazel Fisher
TAKE A DEEP BREATH Margaret O'Neill
HEALING LOVE Meredith Webber

Available from W.H. Smith, John Menzies, Volume One, Forbuoys, Martins, Tesco, Asda, Safeway and other paperback stockists.

Also available from Mills & Boon Reader Service, Freepost, P.O. Box 236, Croydon, Surrey CR9 9EL.

Readers in South Africa - write to:
Book Services International Ltd, P.O. Box 41654, Craighall, Transvaal 2024.

FREE
GOLD PLATED BRACELET

Mills & Boon would like to give you something extra special this Mother's Day—a Gold Plated Bracelet absolutely *FREE* when you purchase a **'Happy Mother's Day'** pack.

The pack features 4 new Romances by popular authors—Victoria Gordon, Debbie Macomber, Joanna Neil and Anne Weale.

Mail-away offer — see pack for details.
Offer closes 31.5.94

Available now   Price £7.20

MILLS & BOON

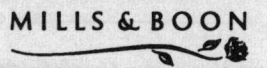

*Available from W. H. Smith, John Menzies, Volume One, Forbuoys, Martins, Tesco, Asda, Safeway and other paperback stockists.
Also available from Mills & Boon Reader Service, FREEPOST, PO Box 236, Croydon, Surrey CR9 9EL. (UK Postage & Packing free)*

FREE BOOK OFFER

HEARTS OF FIRE

By Miranda Lee

HEARTS OF FIRE by Miranda Lee is a totally compelling six-part saga set in Australia's glamorous but cut-throat world of gem dealing.

Discover the passion, scandal, sin and finally the hope that exist between two fabulously rich families. You'll be hooked from the very first page as Gemma Smith fights for the secret of the priceless **Heart of Fire** black opal and fights for love too...

Each novel features a gripping romance in itself. And **SEDUCTION AND SACRIFICE,** the first title in this exciting series, is due for publication in April but you can order your FREE copy, worth £2.50, NOW! To receive your FREE book simply complete the coupon below and return it to:

**MILLS & BOON READER SERVICE, FREEPOST,
P.O. BOX 236, CROYDON CR9 9EL.   TEL: 081-684 2141**

NO STAMP NEEDED

Ms/Mrs/Miss/Mr: _____ HOF

Address _____

_____

_____ Postcode _____

Offer expires 31st. August 1994. One per household. The right is reserved to refuse an application and change the terms of this offer. Offer applies to U.K. and Eire only. Readers overseas please send for details. Southern Africa write to : IBS Private Bag X3010, Randburg 2125. You may be mailed with offers from other reputable companies as a result of this application.
If you would prefer not to receive such offers please tick box ☐

mps MAILING PREFERENCE SERVICE